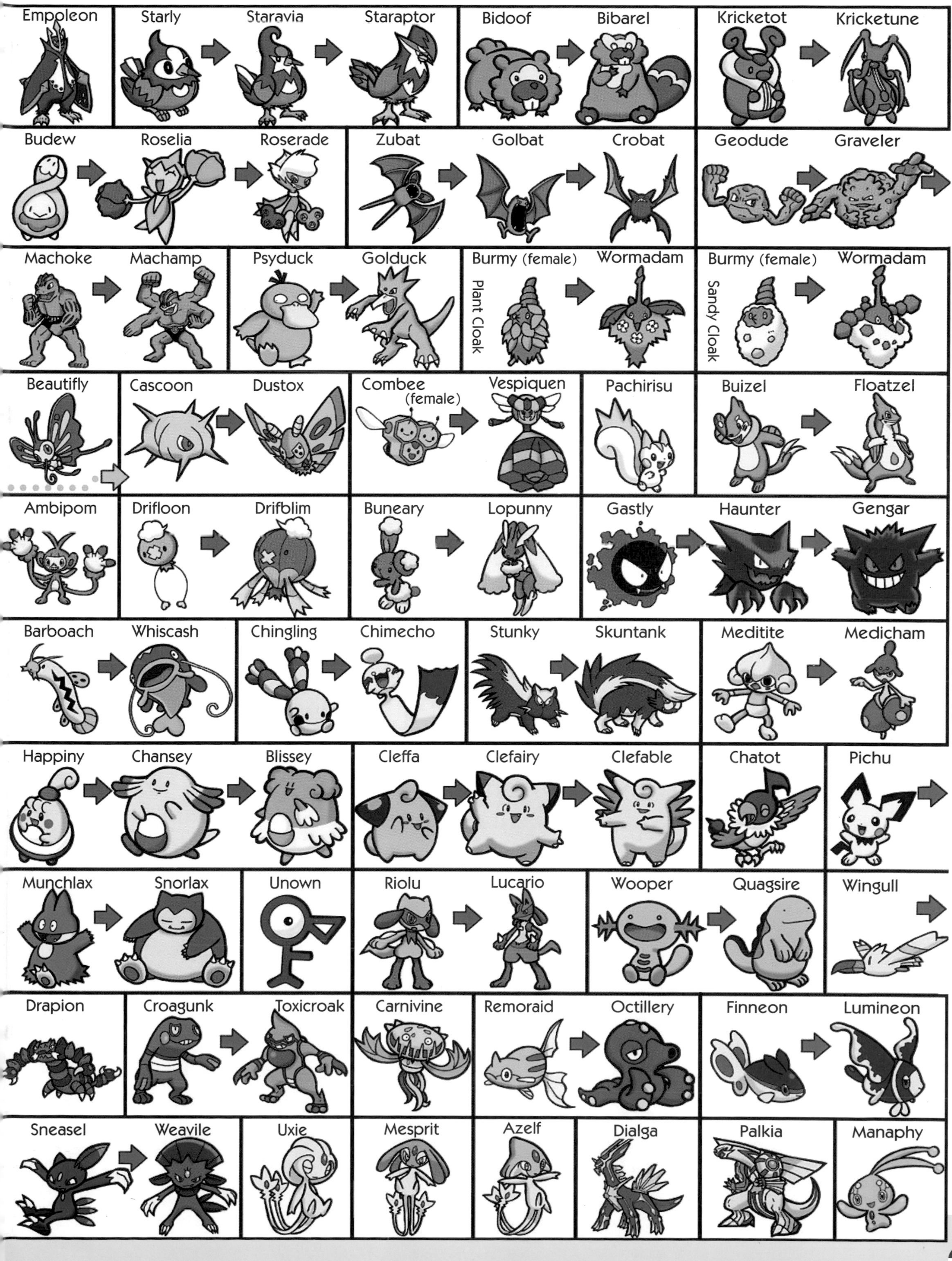

Empoleon
Starly
Staravia
Staraptor
Bidoof
Bibarel
Kricketot
Kricketune
Budew
Roselia
Roserade
Zubat
Golbat
Crobat
Geodude
Graveler
Machoke
Machamp
Psyduck
Golduck
Burmy (female)
Plant Cloak
Wormadam
Burmy (female)
Sandy Cloak
Wormadam
Beautifly
Cascoon
Dustox
Combee
(female)
Vespiquen
Pachirisu
Buizel
Floatzel
Ambipom
Drifloon
Drifblim
Buneary
Lopunny
Gastly
Haunter
Gengar
Barboach
Whiscash
Chingling
Chimecho
Stunky
Skuntank
Meditite
Medicham
Happiny
Chansey
Blissey
Cleffa
Clefairy
Clefable
Chatot
Pichu
Munchlax
Snorlax
Unown
Riolu
Lucario
Wooper
Quagsire
Wingull
Drapion
Croagunk
Toxicroak
Carnivine
Remoraid
Octillery
Finneon
Lumineon
Sneasel
Weavile
Uxie
Mesprit
Azelf
Dialga
Palkia
Manaphy

Let's Greet Everyone on the Way!

- Pass by every Pokémon as you work your way to FINISH.
- Which Pokémon appears twice in this maze?

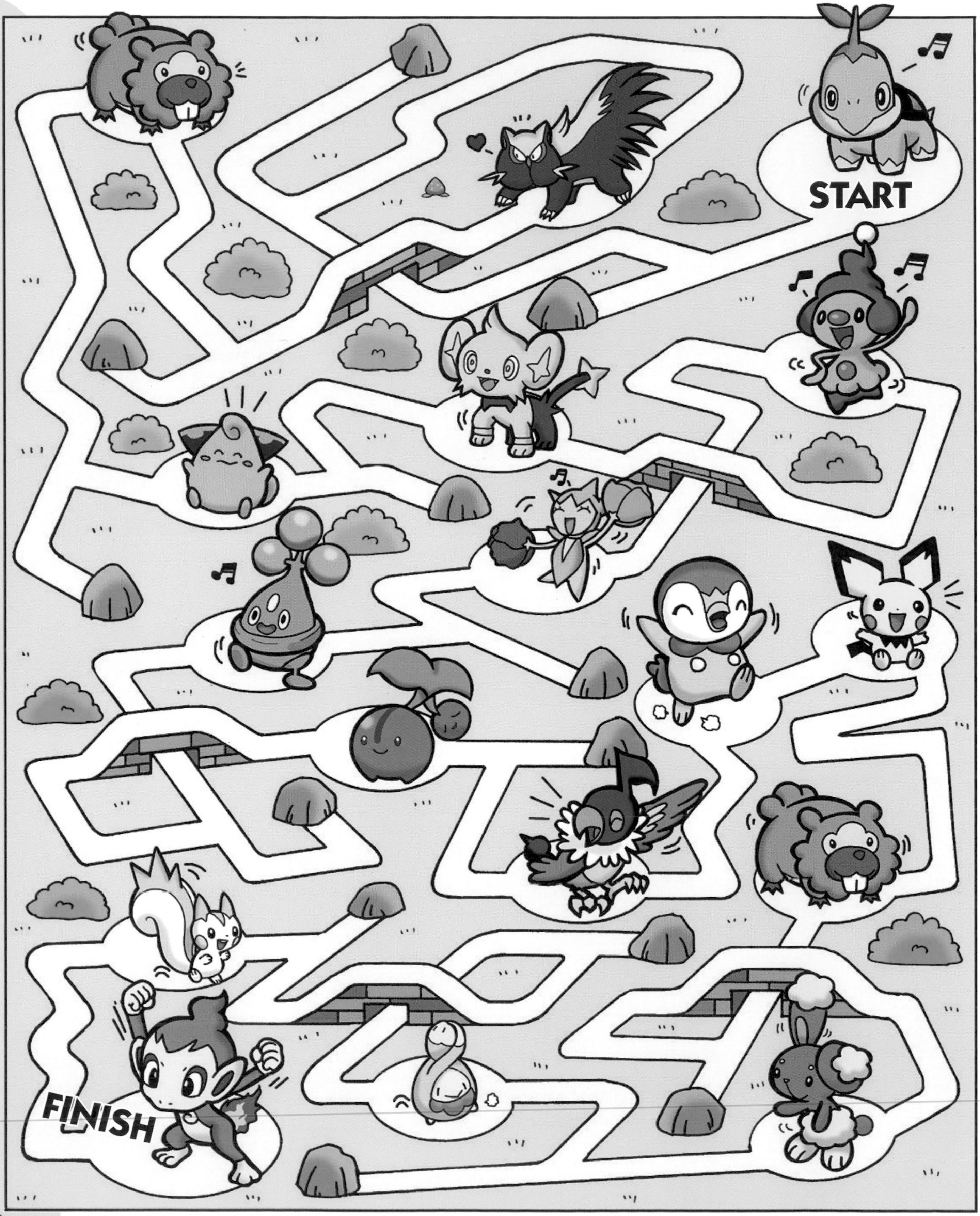
START
FINISH

Cross the Bridge and Finish!

Make it to FINISH by crossing bridges.

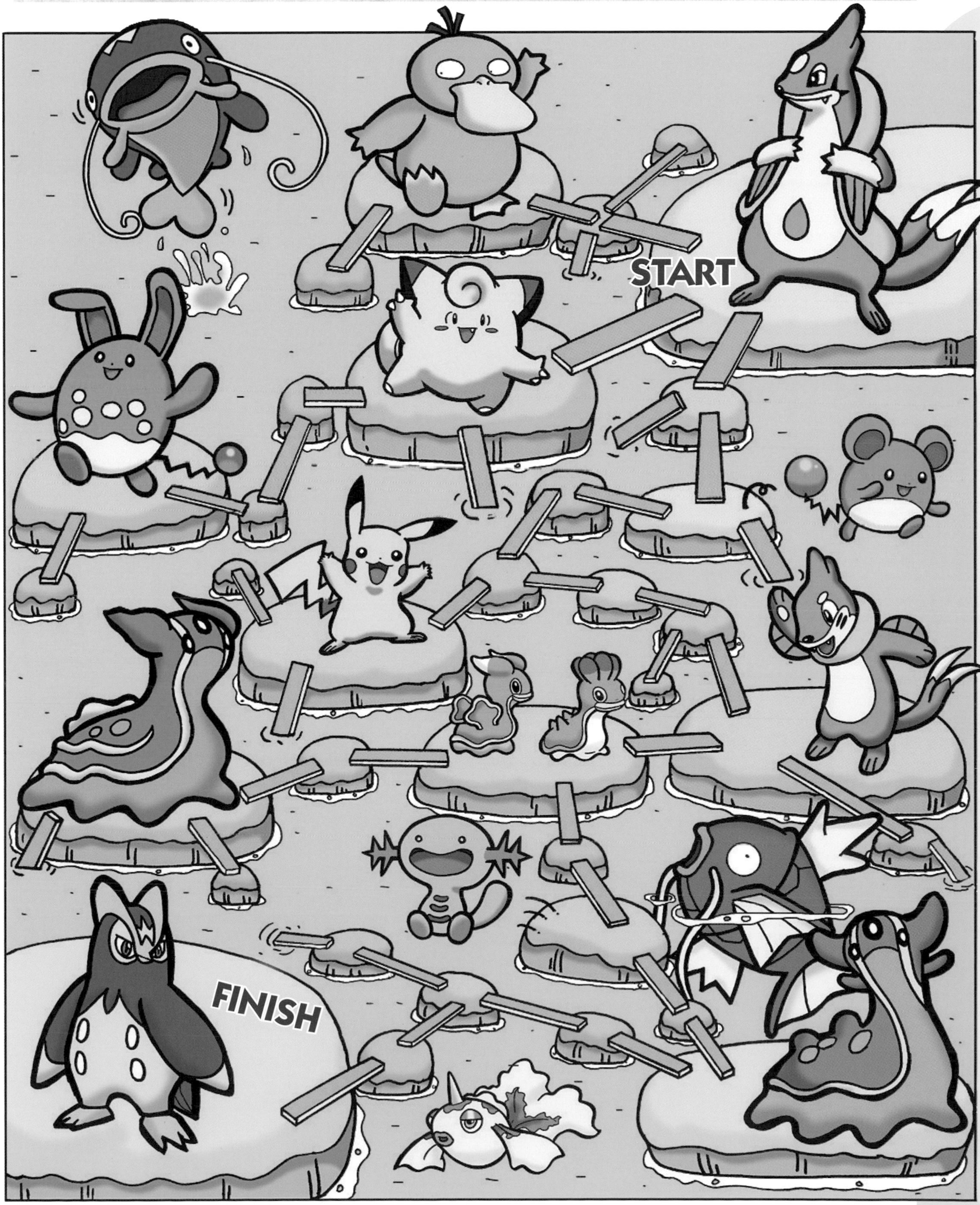

START
FINISH

Let's Climb the Rock Mountain!

Climb up and down the ladders to reach FINISH.
Look at the three Unown shown at the right.
Can you find them in this maze?

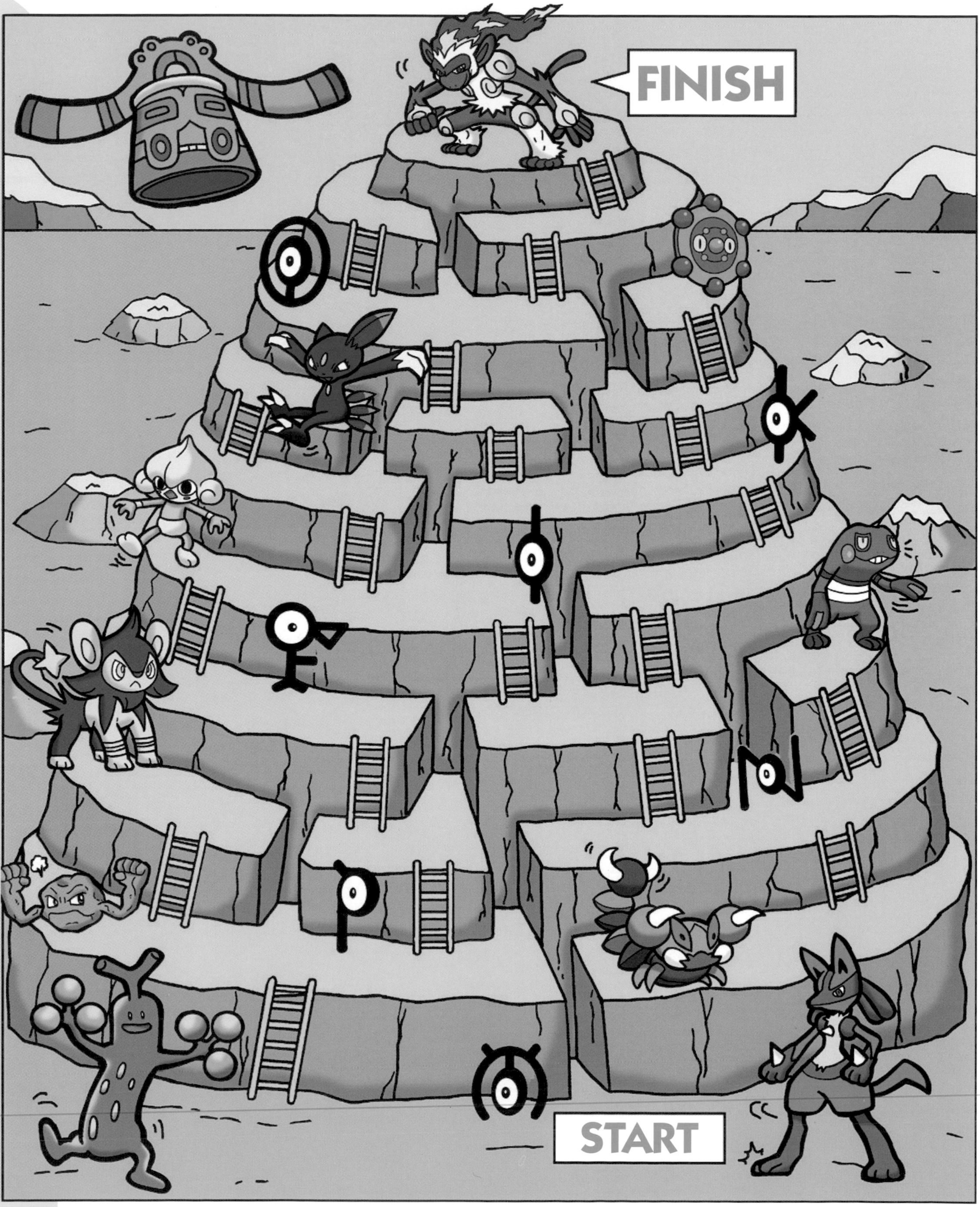

FINISH
START

The Most Pokémon

Which Pokémon appears most often in this picture?

Budew Starly Kricketot Pachirisu Cherubi Wurmple

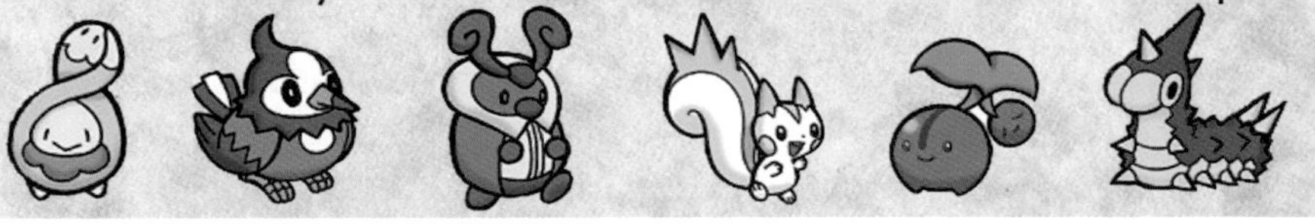

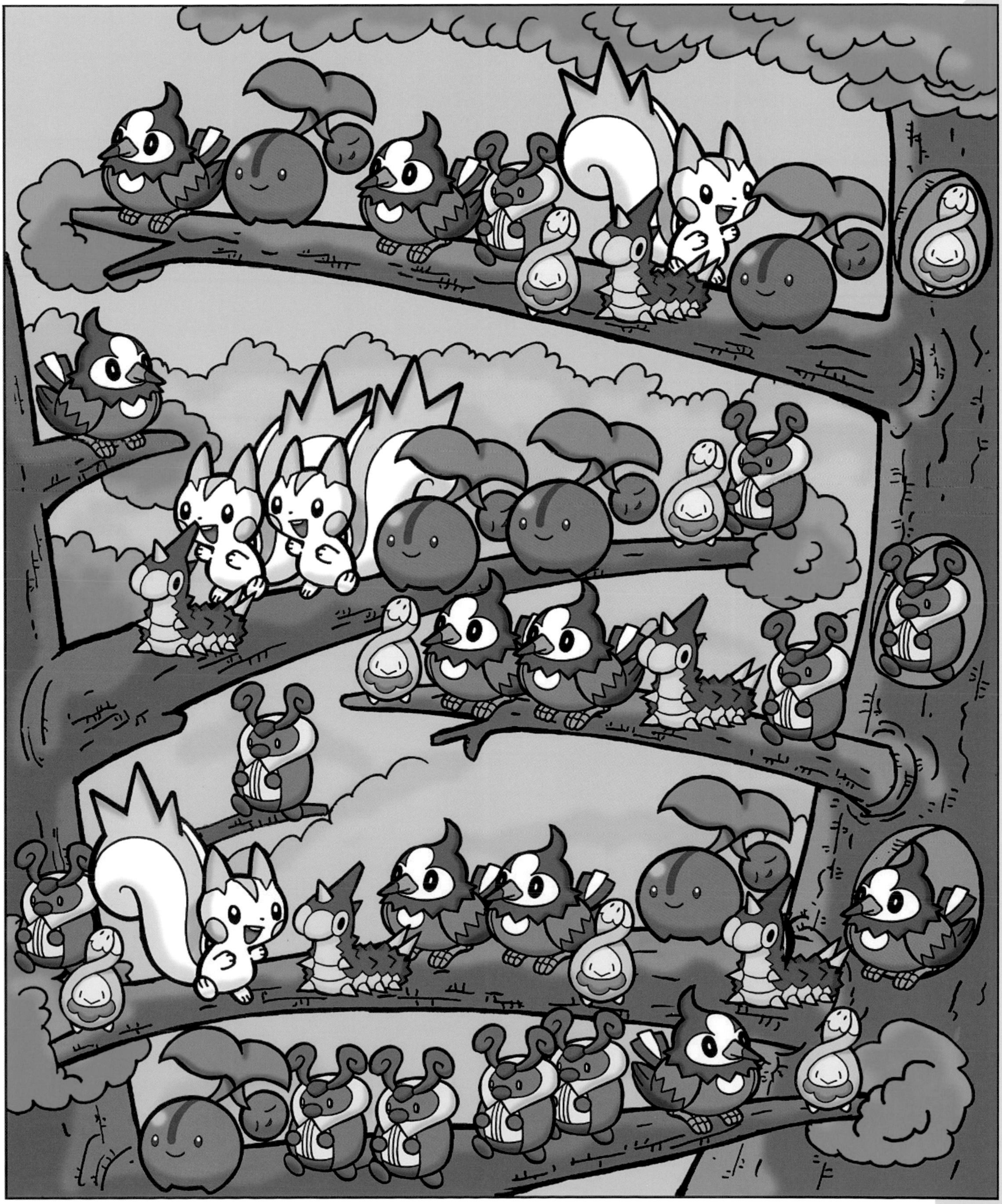

Let's Avoid Gible!

- Can you make it from START to FINISH without running into Gible?
- How many Pichu have this face in this maze?

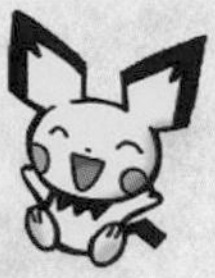

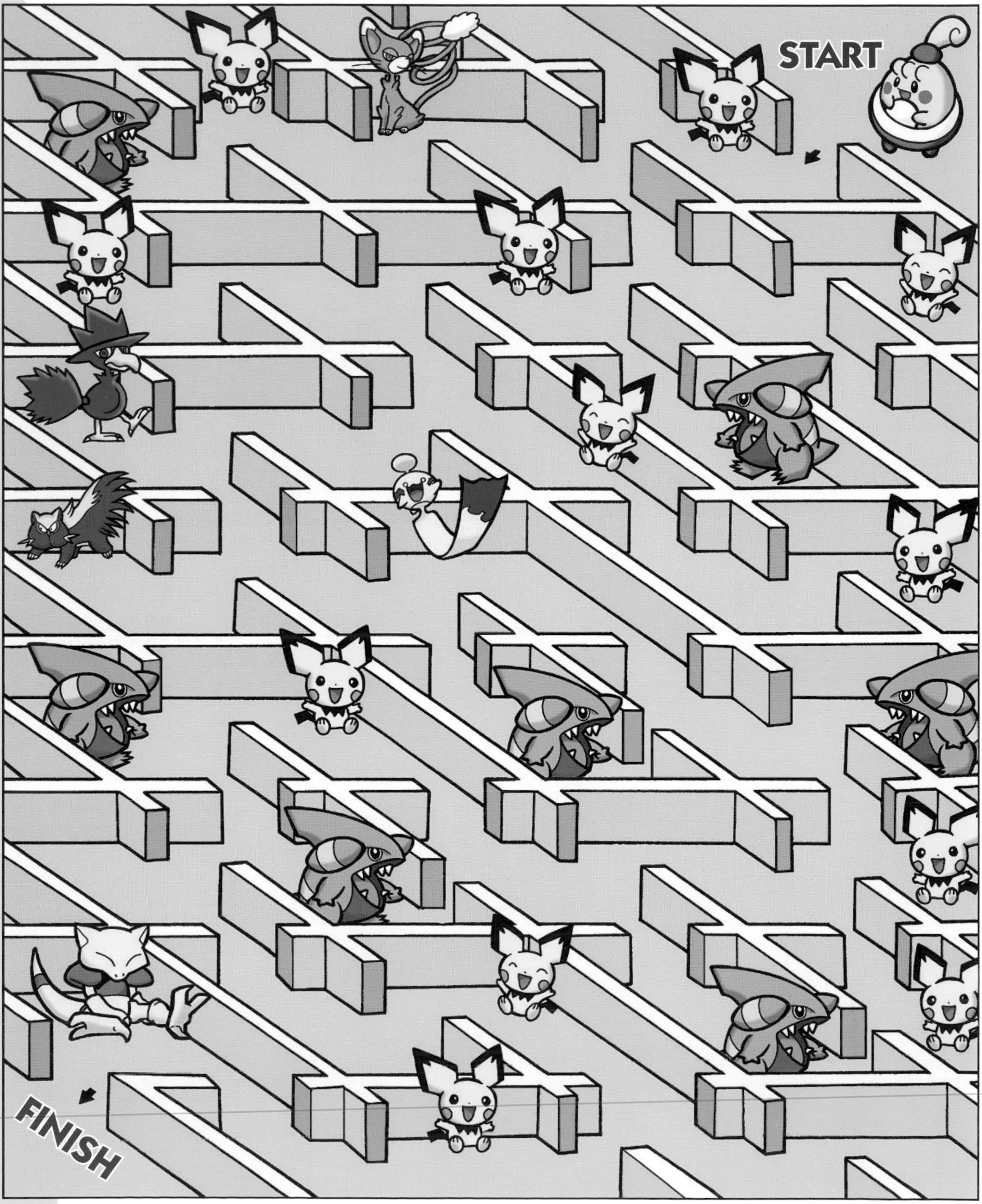
START
FINISH

Let's Swim to Finish!

- This maze is in the sea. Find your way from START to FINISH.
- There are 12 Finneon 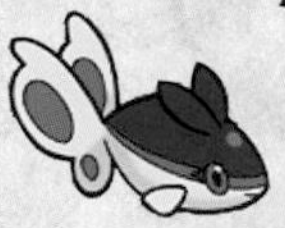 in this maze. Can you find them all?

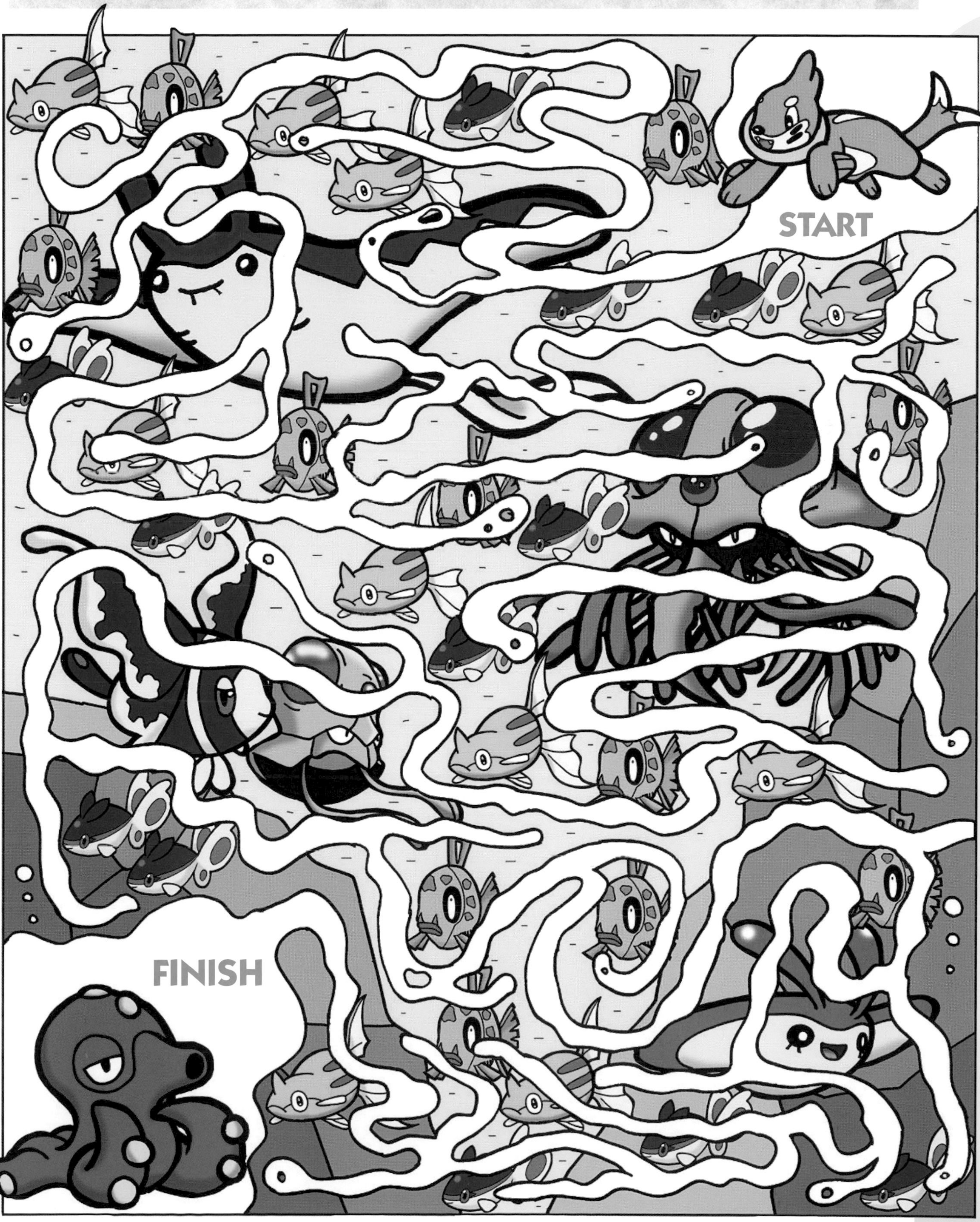
START
FINISH

Find the Evolved Pokémon!

Pokémon were playing in a field when four of them evolved! Can you find the four evolved Pokémon in the picture on the right page?

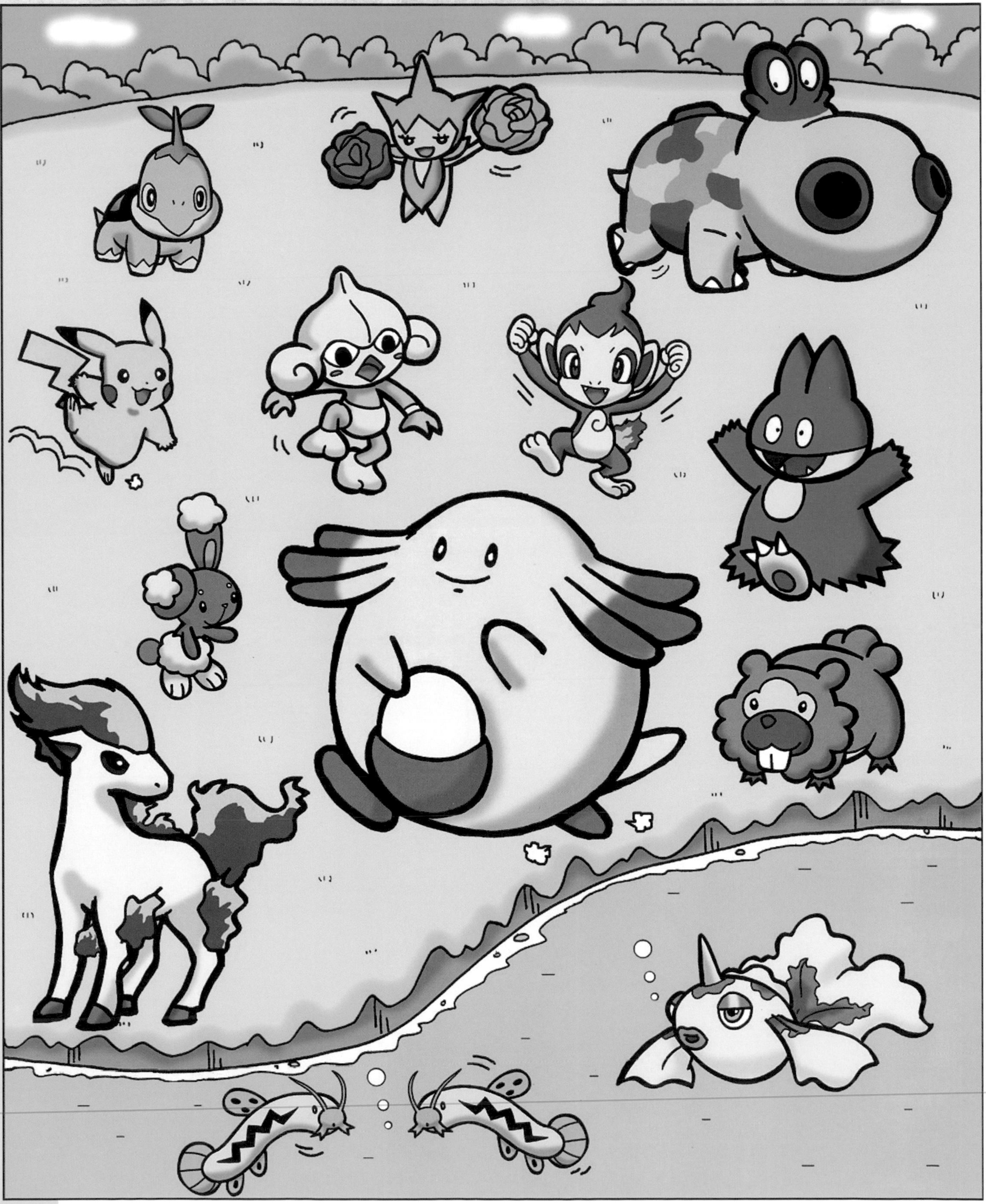

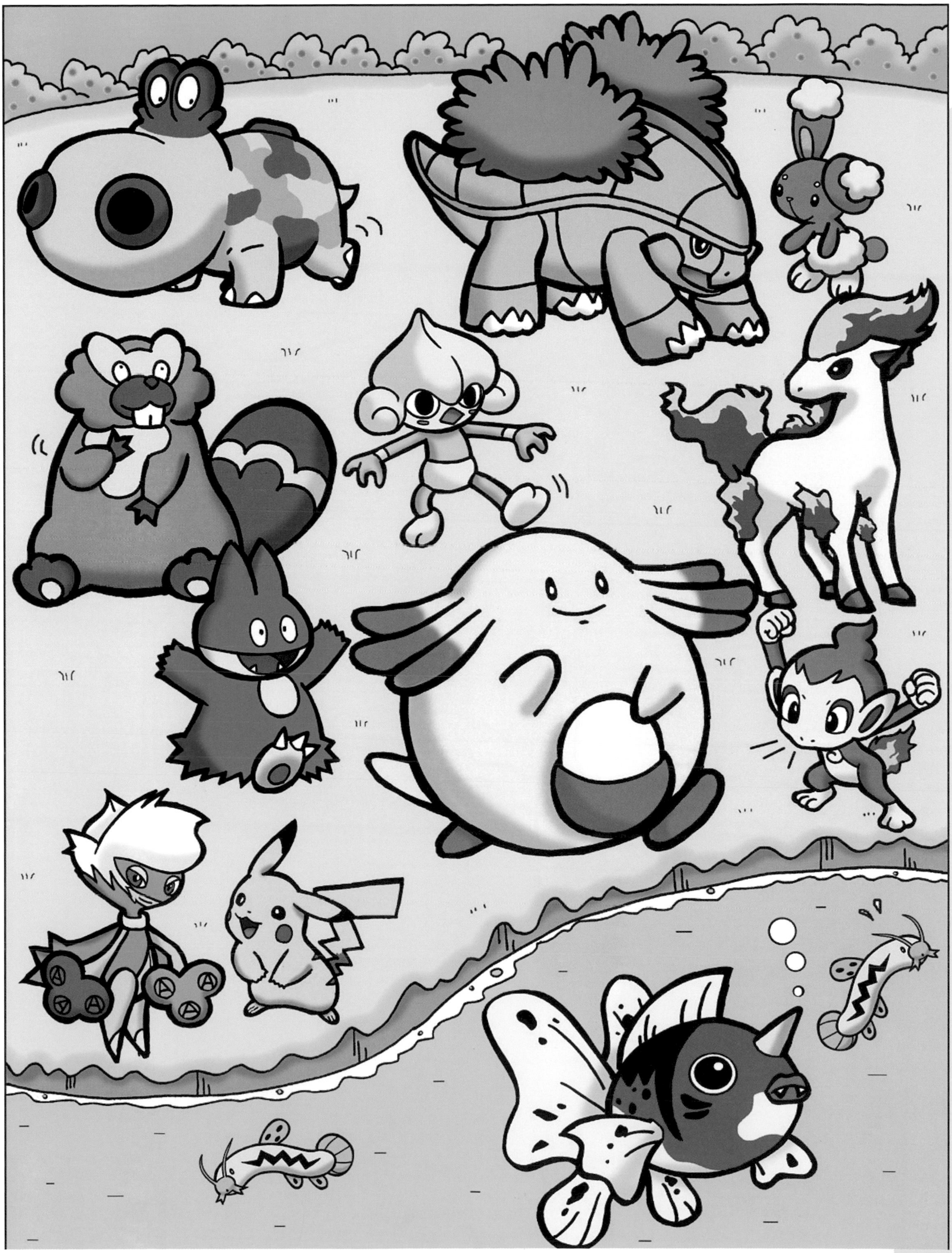

Cloud Maze

- Walk through the cloud and find your way to FINISH.
- There is only one Pokémon you don't pass by on the way to FINISH. Which Pokémon is it?

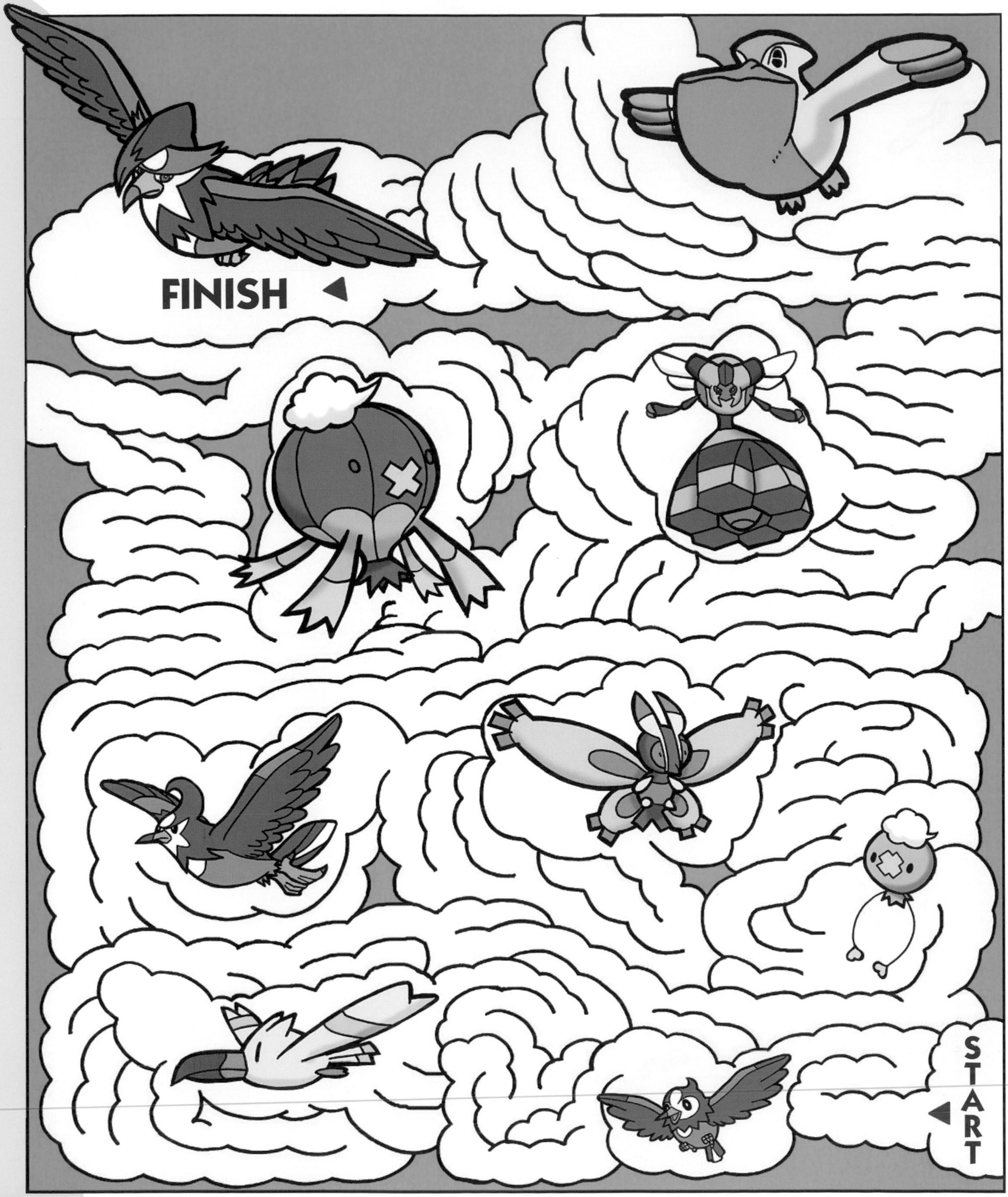

FINISH
START

Fun with Japanese!

Here's a puzzle that uses Pokémon names—in Japanese! Follow the line from START. As you pass through each square, take the first Japanese letter of each Pokémon name. When you reach the end, put all the letters together. Which Pokémon do you get? 1, 2, or 3?

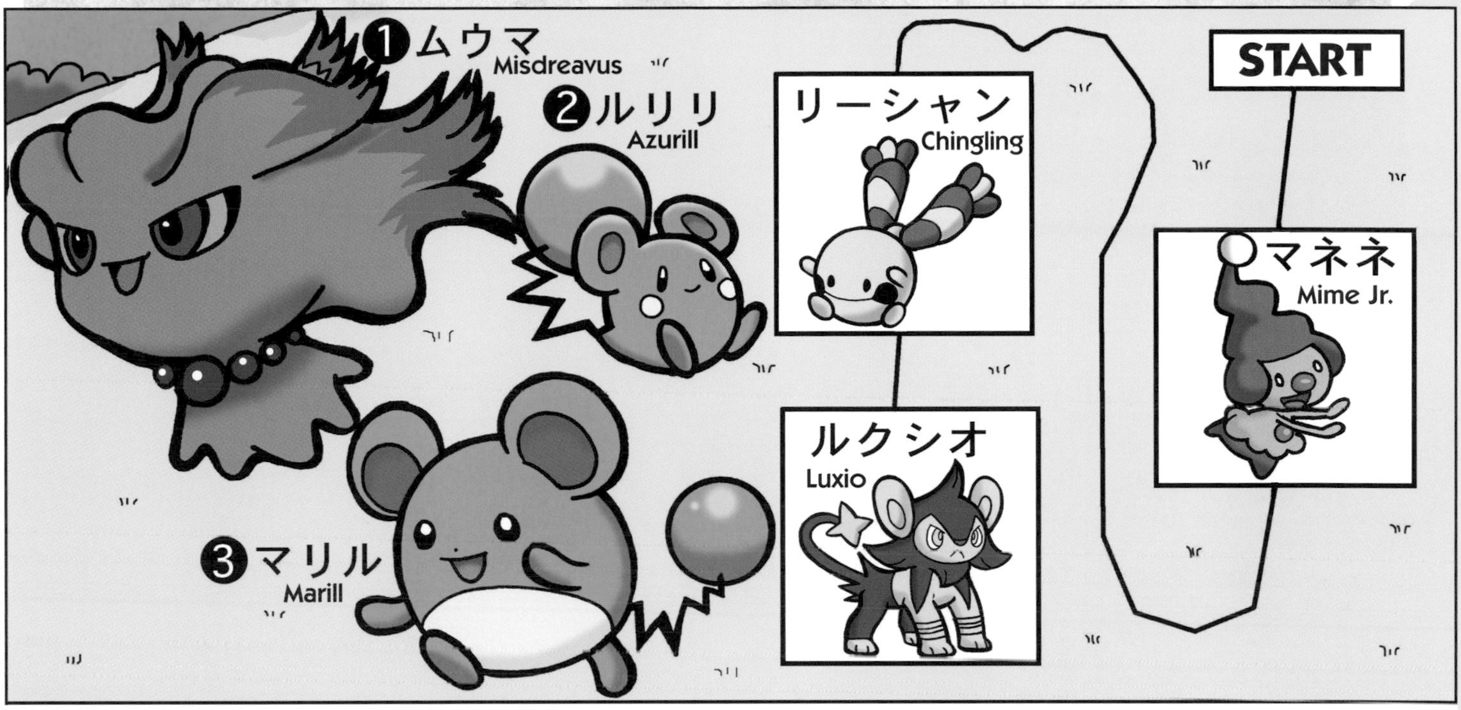

START
マネネ
Mime Jr.
リーシャン
Chingling
ルクシオ
Luxio
1 ムウマ
Misdreavus
2 ルリリ
Azurill
3 マリル
Marill

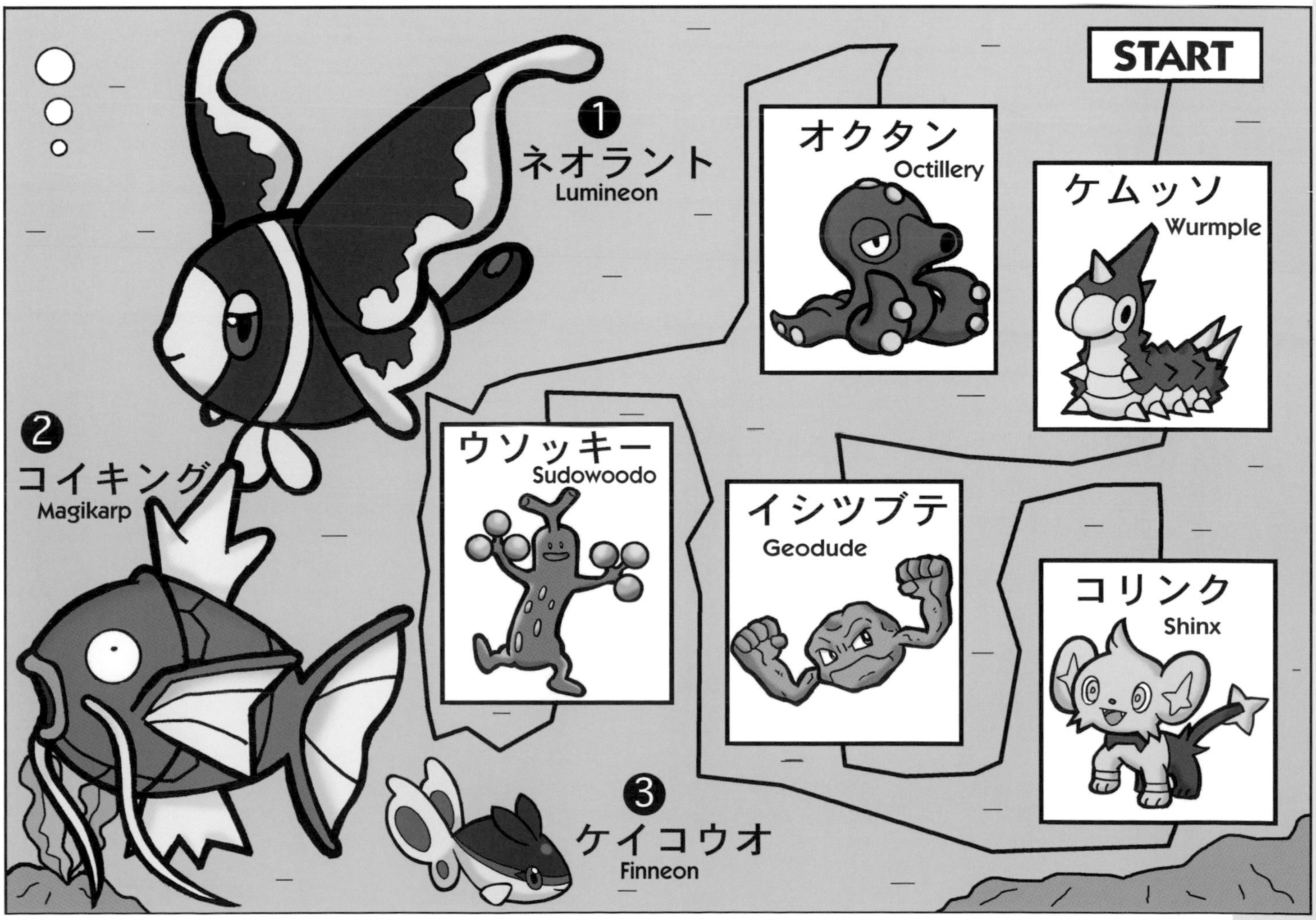

START
ケムッソ
Wurmple
オクタン
Octillery
コリンク
Shinx
イシツブテ
Geodude
ウソッキー
Sudowoodo
1 ネオラント
Lumineon
2 コイキング
Magikarp
3 ケイコウオ
Finneon

Let's Walk Around Budew!

Which Pokémon walks around five Budew before reaching FINISH?

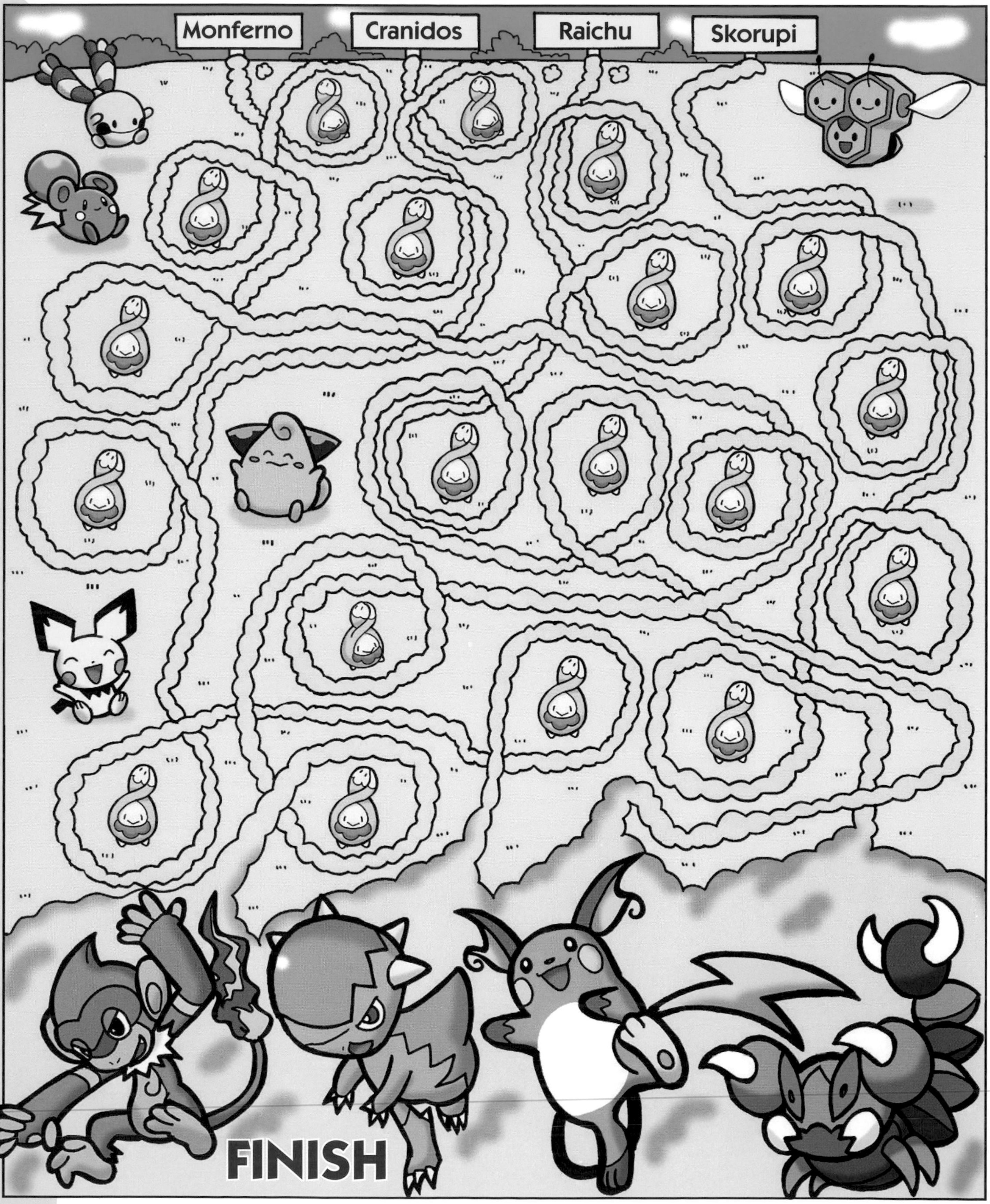

Monferno
Cranidos
Raichu
Skorupi
FINISH

Let's Play a Japanese Word Game!

● In the START square, you'll find Pokémon's name spelled in Japanese. In order to move to the next square, the last Japanese letter of the Pokémon's name must match the first Japanese letter in the next square. Keep going all the way to FINISH!

START

スカンプー Stunky	キャモメ Wingull	Girafarig キリンリキ	ウソッキー Sudowoodo	ピカチュウ Pikachu
パチリス Pachirisu	マスキッパ Carnivine	Misdreavus ムウマ	チェリム Cherrim	ウソハチ Bonsly
Octillery オクタン	リーシャン Chingling	マネネ Mime Jr.	ムックル Starly	チリーン Chimecho
Remoraid テッポウオ	トキサント Goldeen	ネオラント Lumineon	トリデプス Bastiodon	スボミー Budew
イソツブテ Geodude	ピィ Cleffa	ピッピ Clefairy	スコルピ Skorupi	ミノムッチ Burmy
Gastrodon トリトドン (West Sea) (East Sea)	クロバット Crobat	ピンプク Happiny	チャーレム Medicham
	ドラピオン Drapion	ドータクン Bronzong	ムクバード Staravia

FINISH

15

One Less or One More

Move to a spot that has one more or one less Pokémon than the spot you are in to move to FINISH.

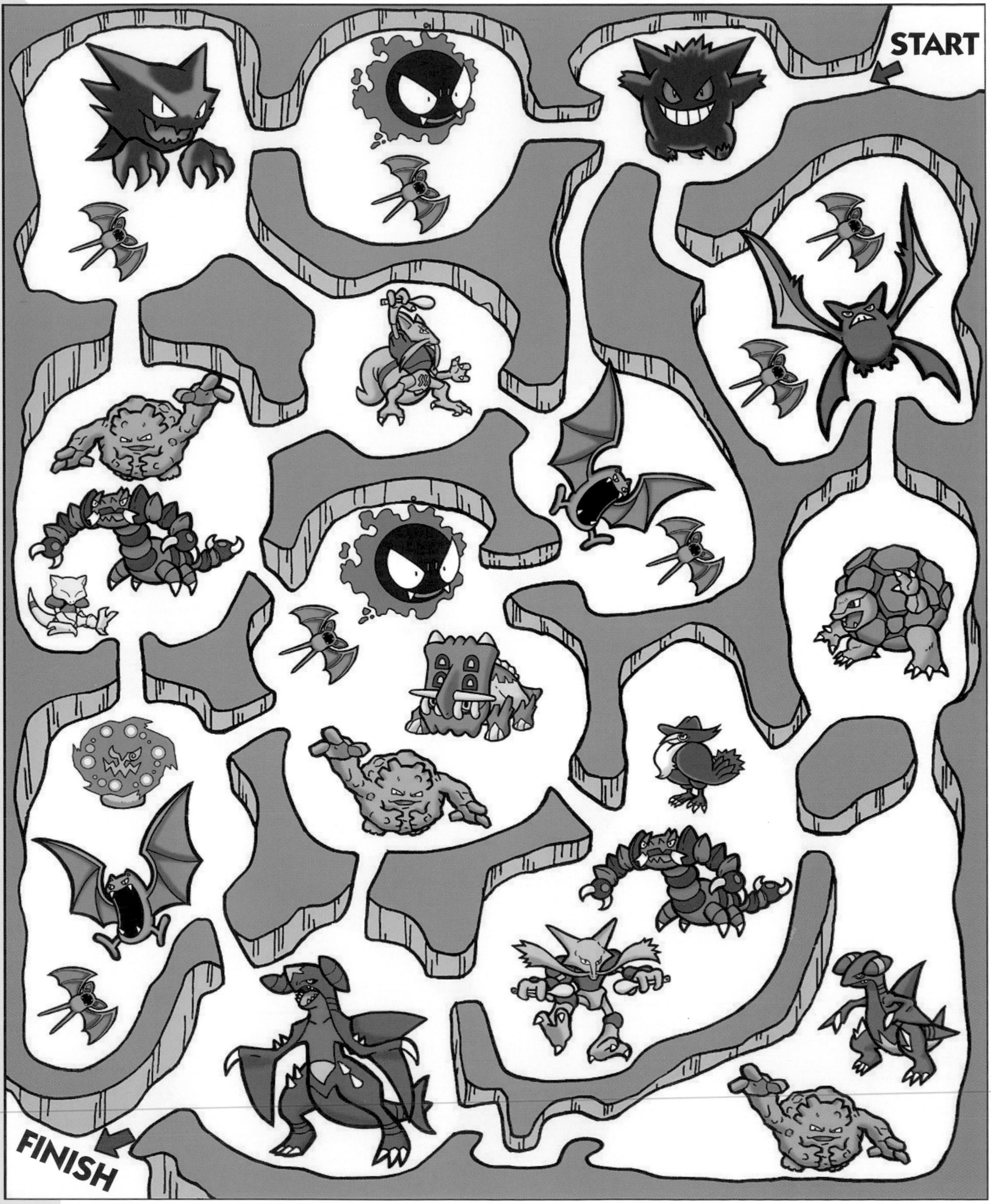
START
FINISH

Who Will Collect the Most Nuts?

Which Pokémon will collect the most nuts before reaching Cherrim?

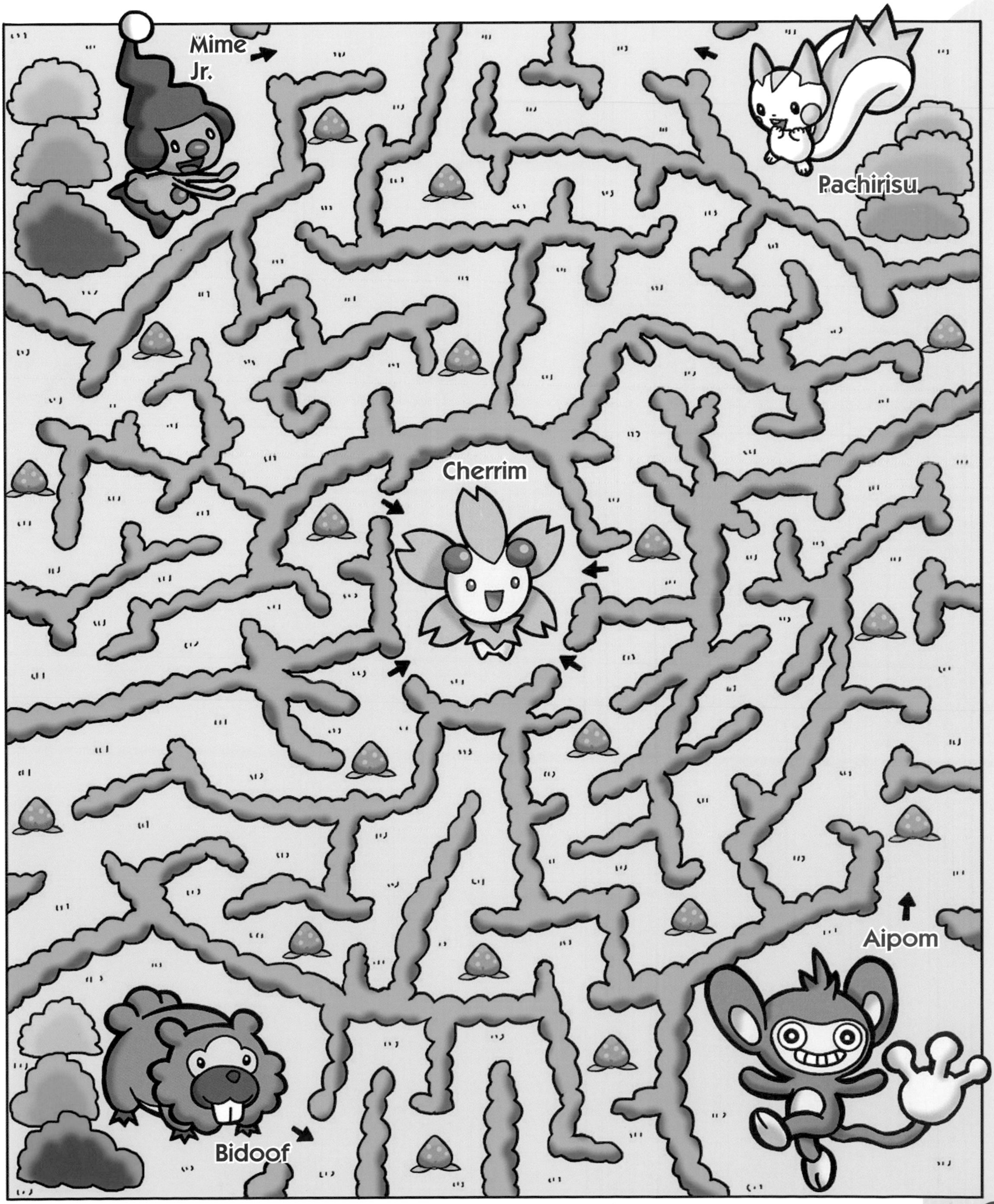
Mime Jr.
Pachirisu
Cherrim
Aipom
Bidoof

Pikachu's 100,000 Volts!

- Find your way out from START to FINISH.
- Can you find the matching silhouette for each of the Pokémon, 1 through 8?
- Which is the fifth Pokémon to be hit by Pikachu's electricity?

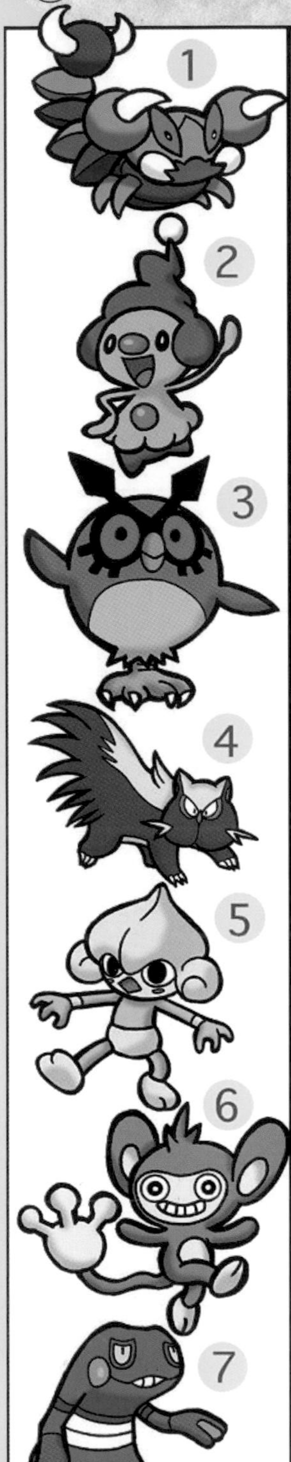
1
2
3
4
5
6
7
8

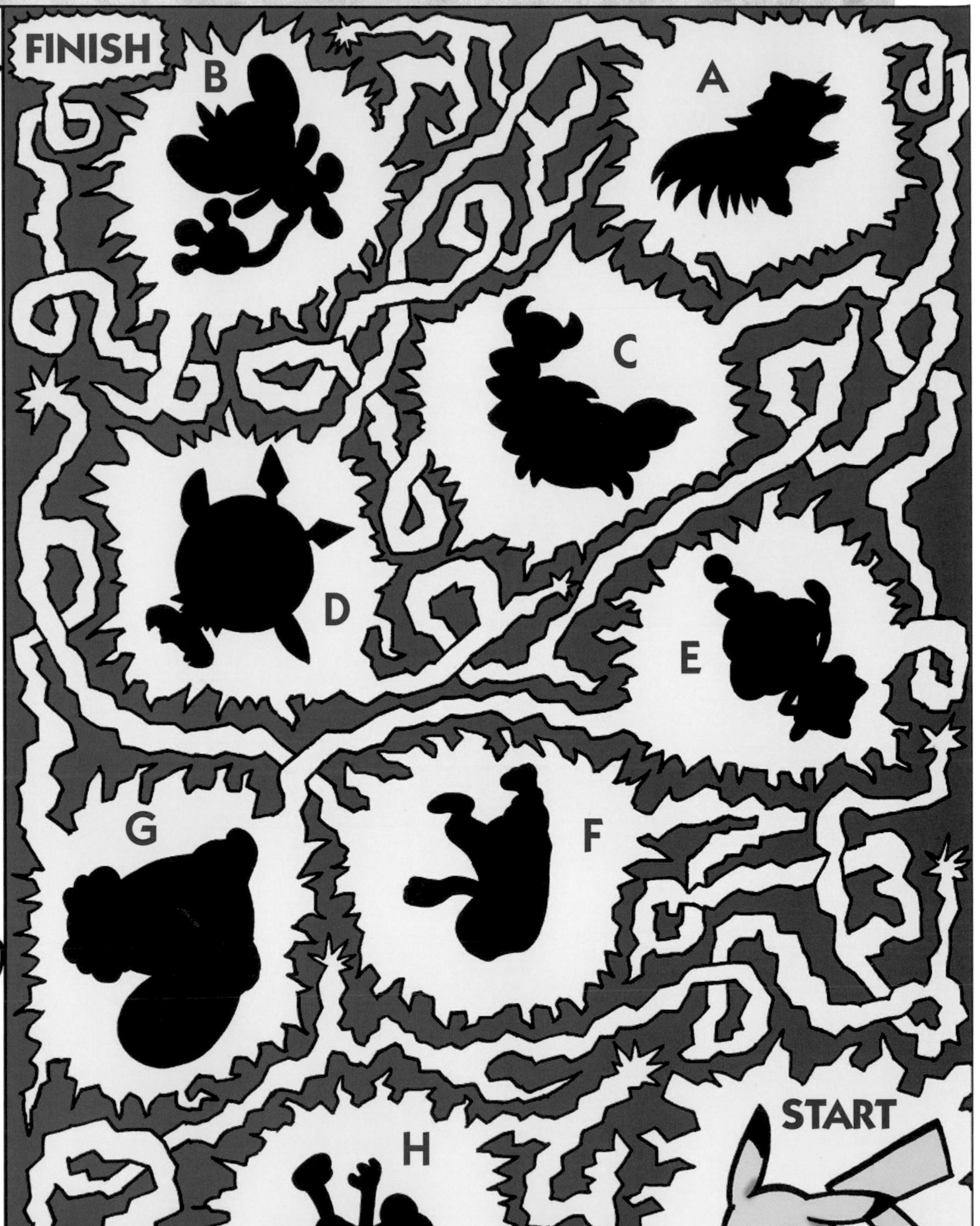
FINISH
B
A
C
D
E
G
F
H
START

Let's Move in Order!

Make your way through the maze in the order of Uxie → Mesprit → Azelf. Which Pokémon will you reach in the end?

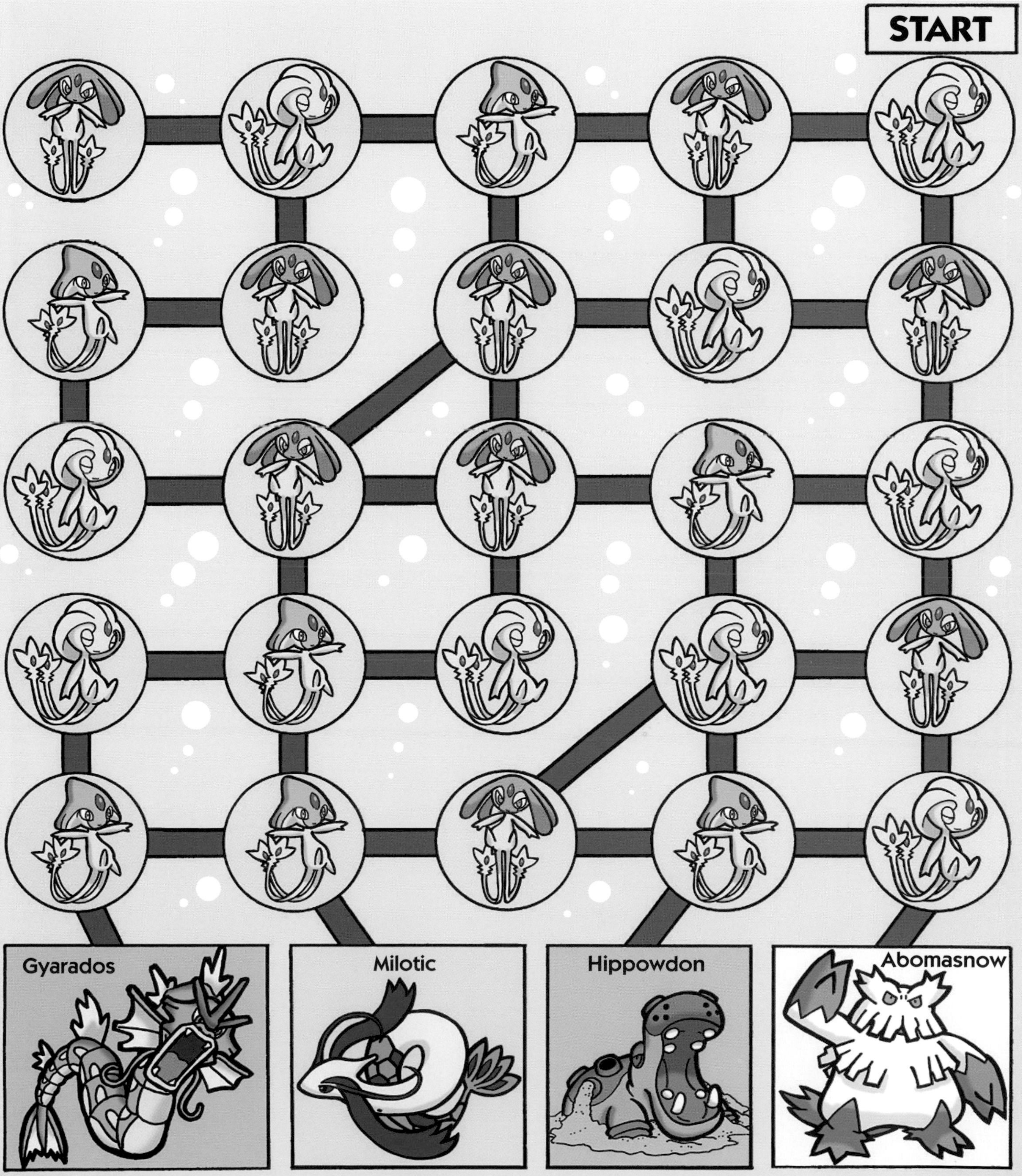

START
Gyarados
Milotic
Hippowdon
Abomasnow

Who's Missing?

Some Pokémon are gathered on top of a mountain. There are three Pokémon in the picture on the left who are missing from the picture on the right. Can you name the three missing Pokémon?

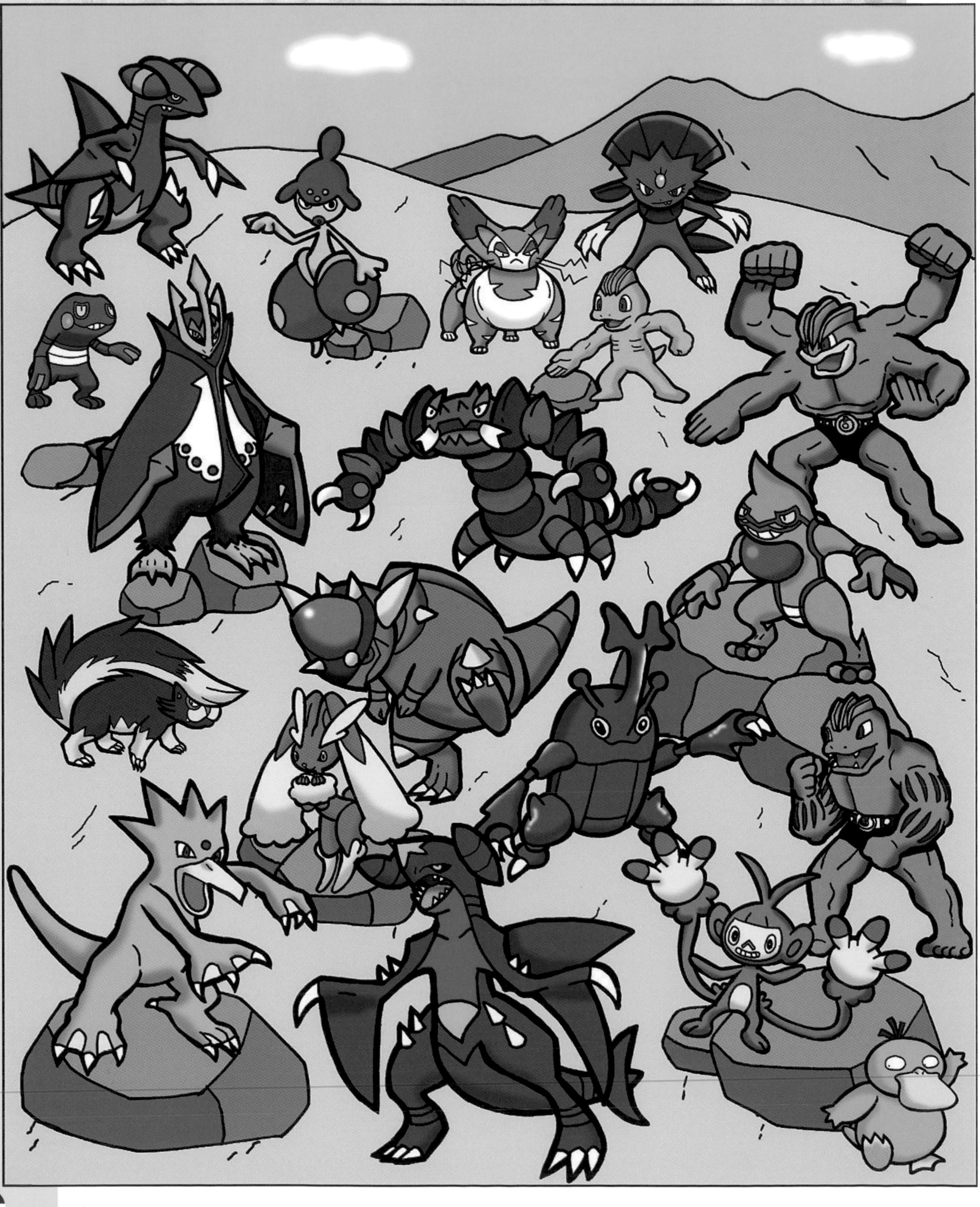

Four new Pokémon have joined the others in the picture below. Can you name these Pokémon?

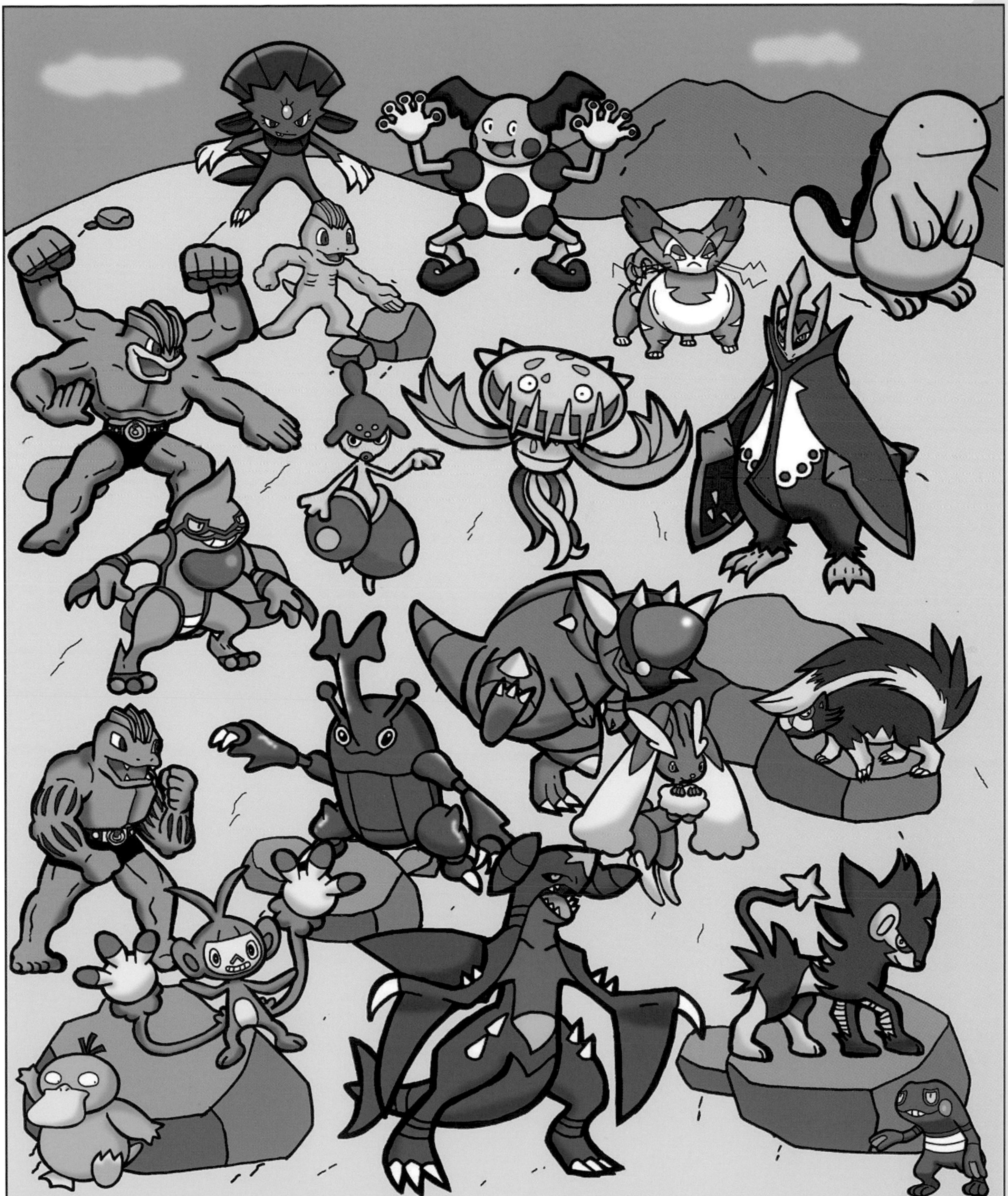

Brick Maze

Pass by each of the Pokémon in the maze as you proceed to FINISH.

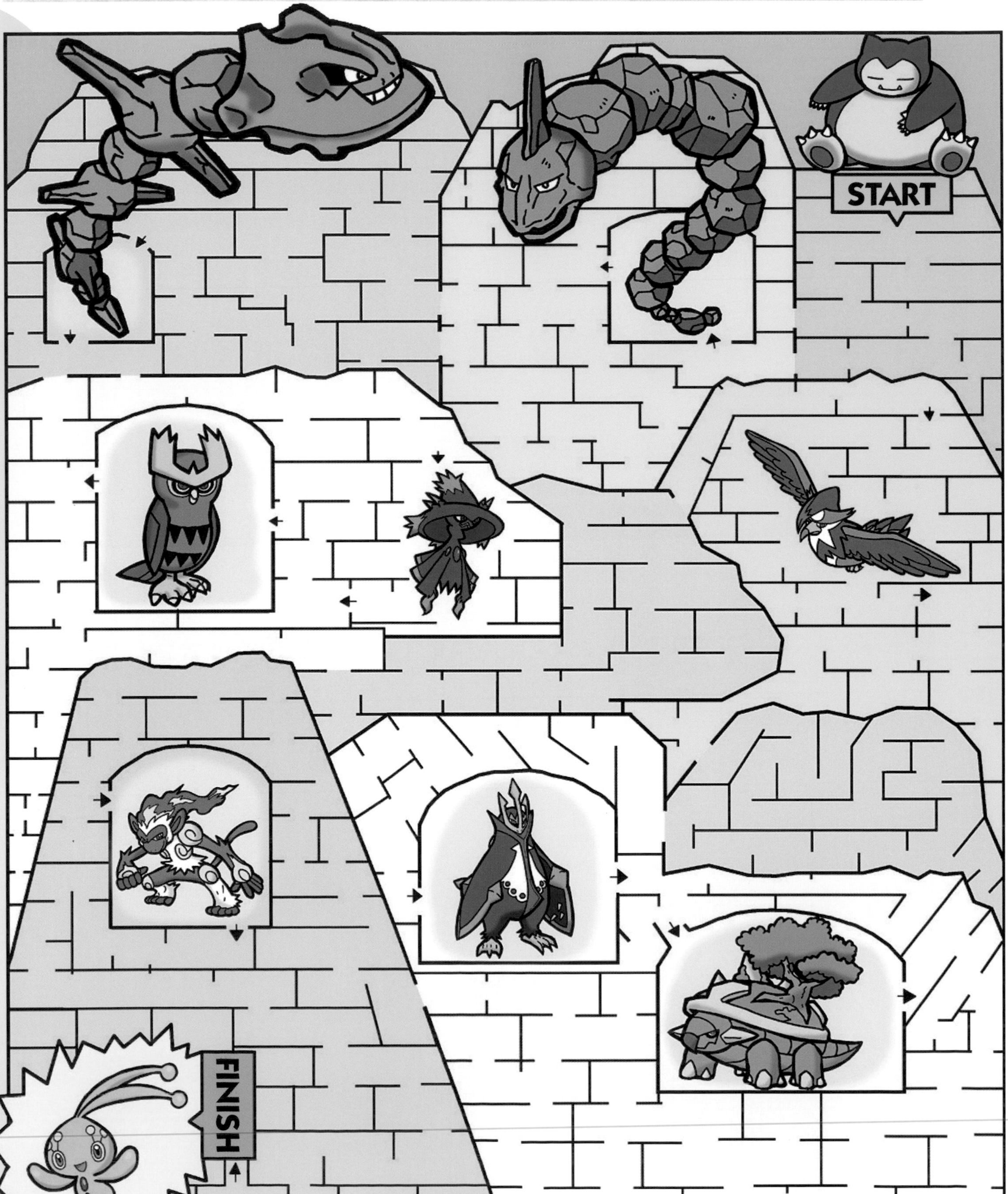

START
FINISH

Who Will Meet the Most Pokémon?

Can you find which Pokémon will meet the most Pokémon as they move through the pipe maze?

Pipe Maze Rules

Start from the top and go down. Every time you come to a corner, you must turn.

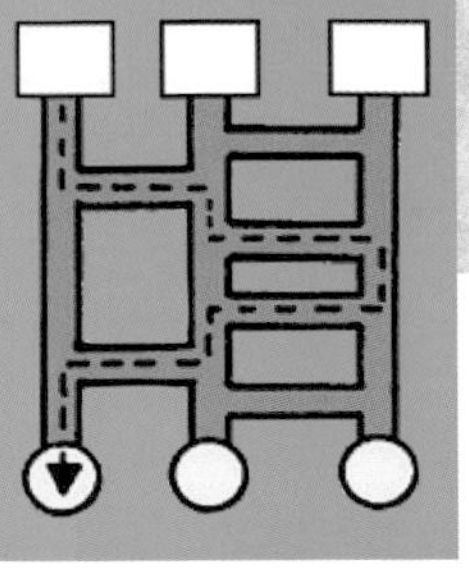

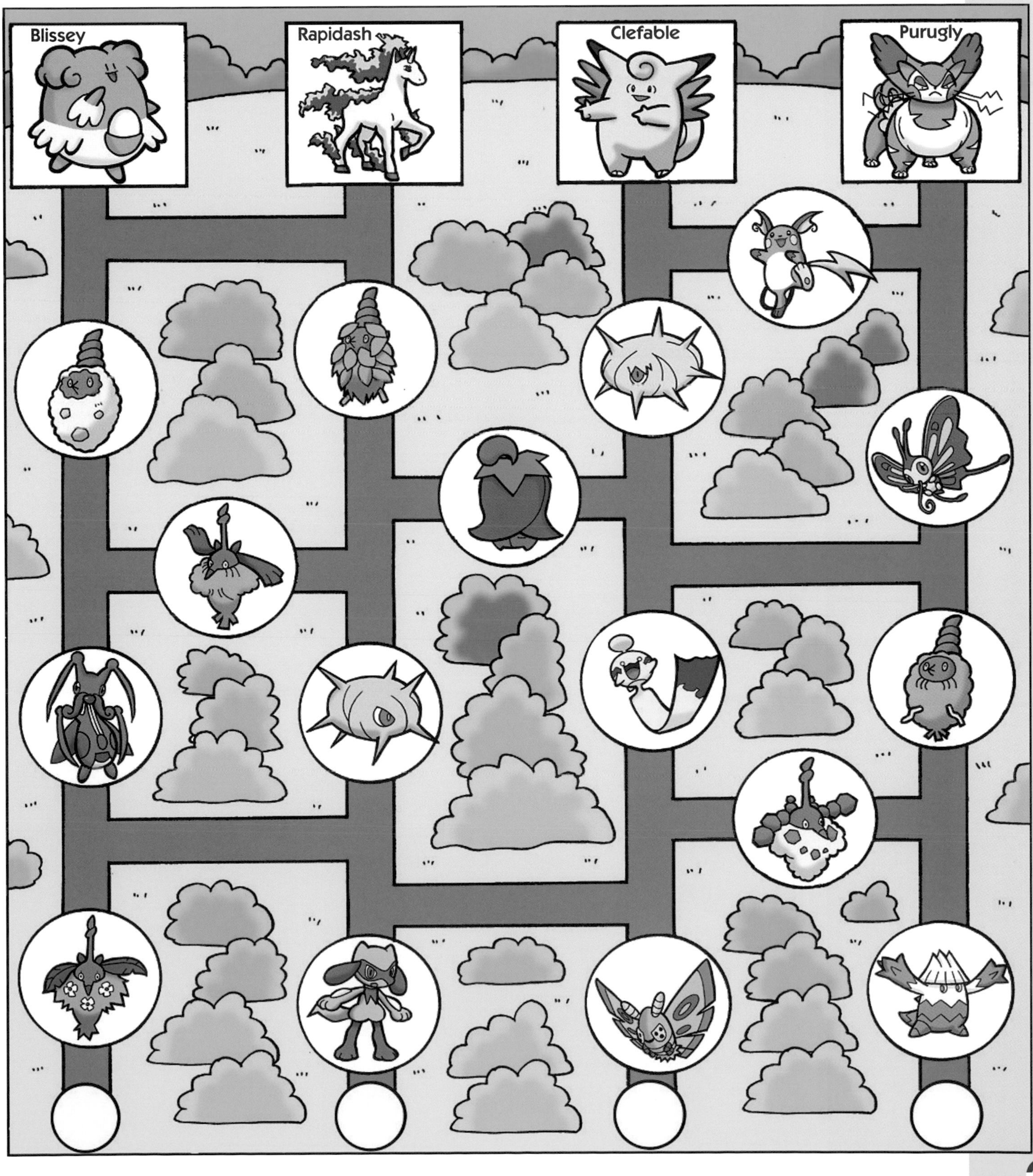

Blissey
Rapidash
Clefable
Purugly

Right or Wrong?

◉ Choose the right answer in each box to reach FINISH.

START

① Which Pokémon can use an Attack Move called "Leaf Cutter"?

Bonsly

Turtwig

② Which one is the "Head Butt" Pokémon?

Shieldon

Cranidos

Sorry, wrong answer. Start over.

③ Which legs belong to Snover?

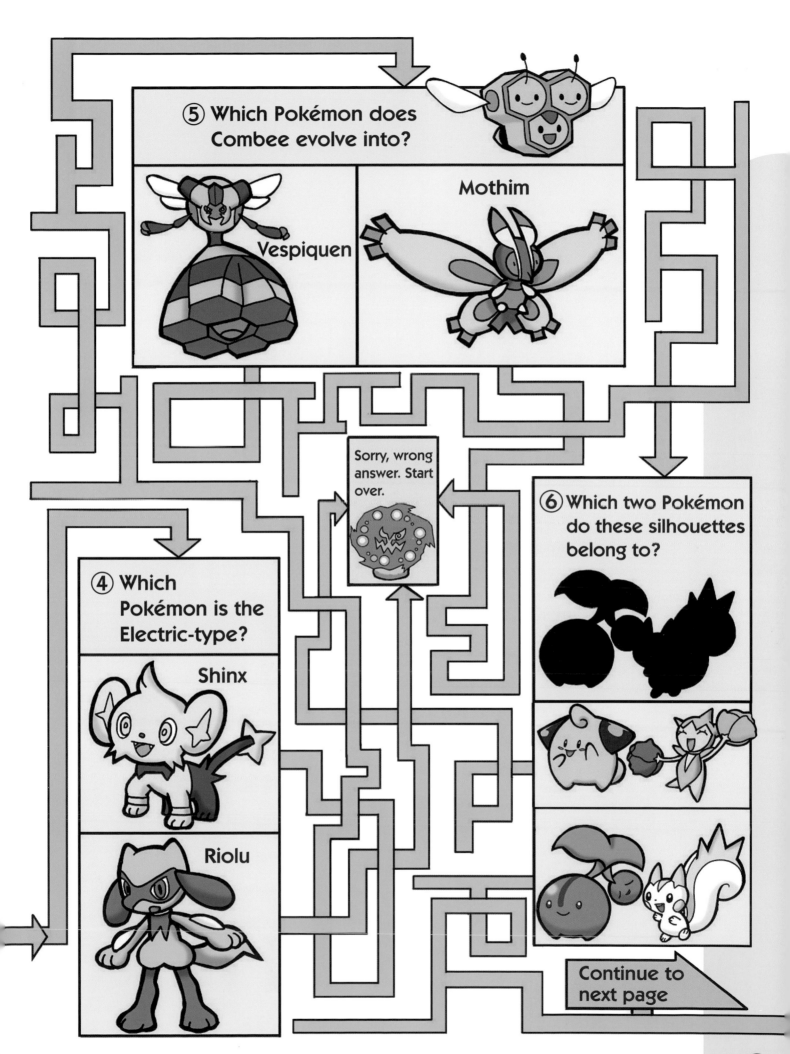

⑤ Which Pokémon does Combee evolve into?

Vespiquen

Mothim

Sorry, wrong answer. Start over.

④ Which Pokémon is the Electric-type?

Shinx

Riolu

⑥ Which two Pokémon do these silhouettes belong to?

Continue to next page

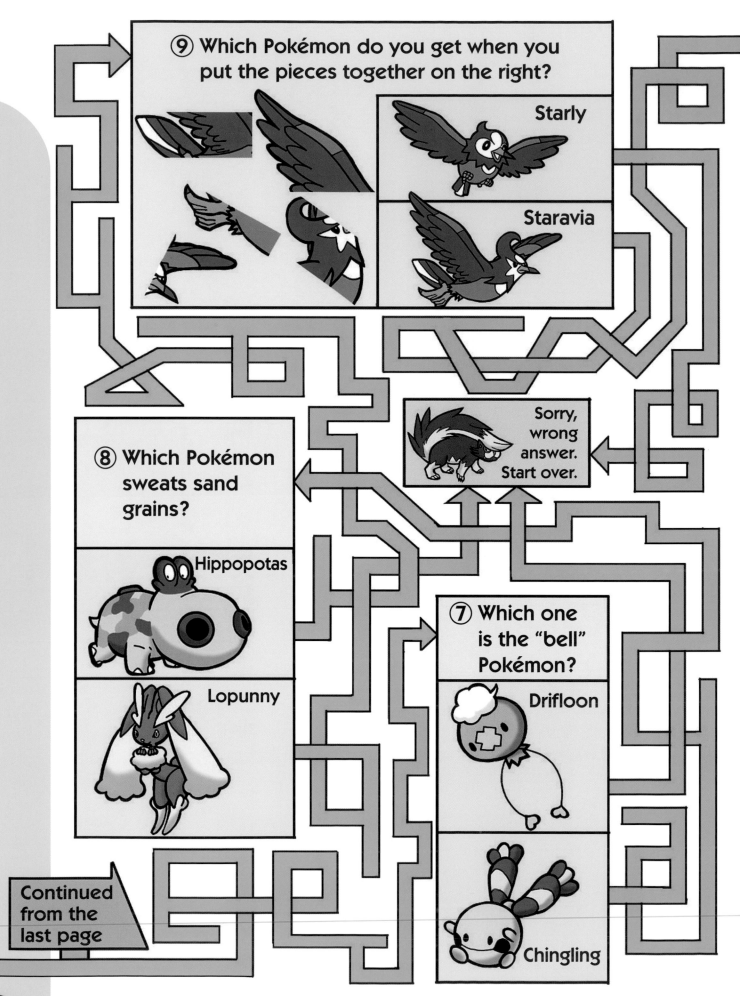

⑨ Which Pokémon do you get when you put the pieces together on the right?

Starly

Staravia

Sorry, wrong answer. Start over.

⑧ Which Pokémon sweats sand grains?

Hippopotas

Lopunny

⑦ Which one is the "bell" Pokémon?

Drifloon

Chingling

Continued from the last page

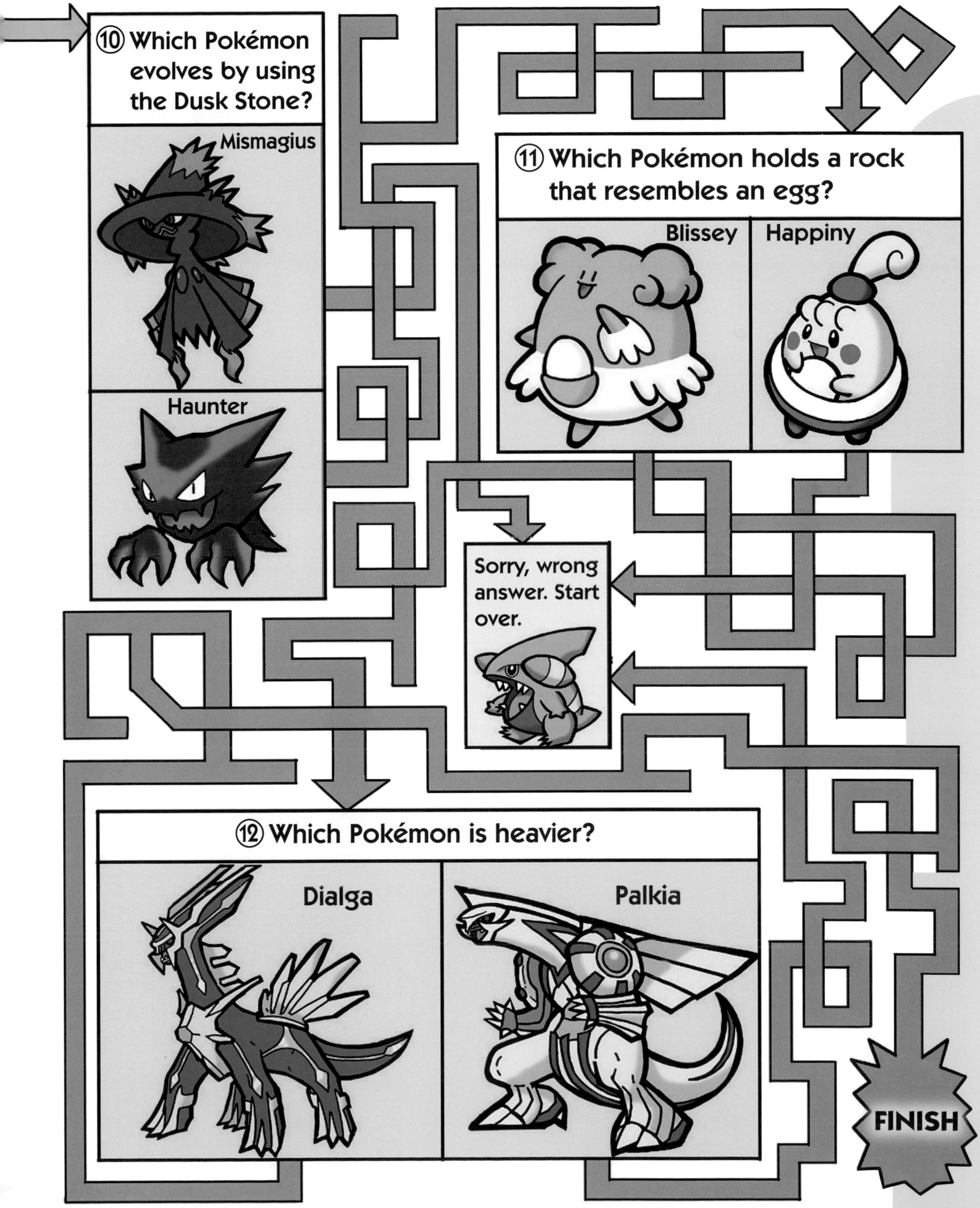
⑩ Which Pokémon evolves by using the Dusk Stone?
Mismagius
Haunter
⑪ Which Pokémon holds a rock that resembles an egg?
Blissey
Happiny
Sorry, wrong answer. Start over.
⑫ Which Pokémon is heavier?
Dialga
Palkia
FINISH

Answers

Cover Mazes

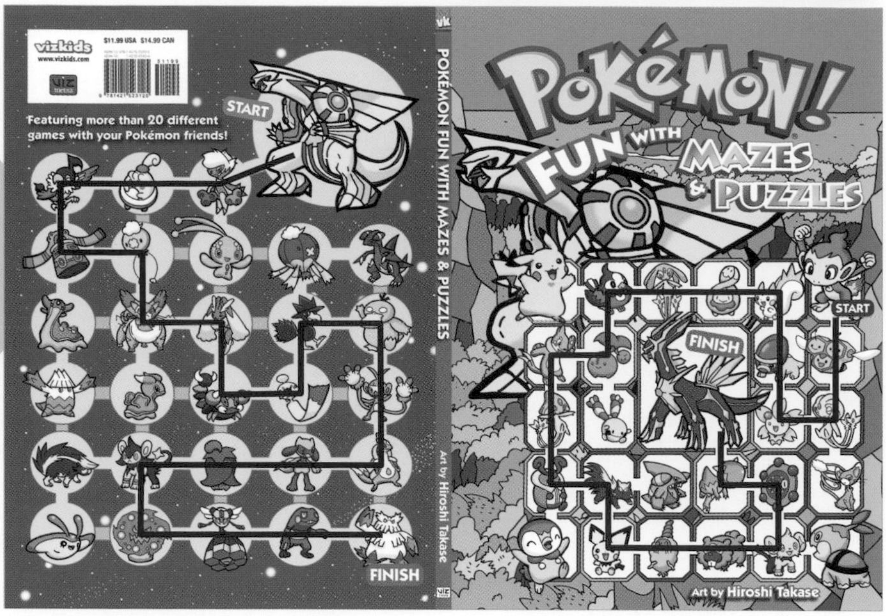

Featuring more than 20 different games with your Pokémon friends!
START
FINISH
POKÉMON FUN WITH MAZES & PUZZLES
Art by Hiroshi Takase
POKÉMON! FUN WITH MAZES & PUZZLES
START
FINISH
Art by Hiroshi Takase

Let's Greet Everyone on the Way!

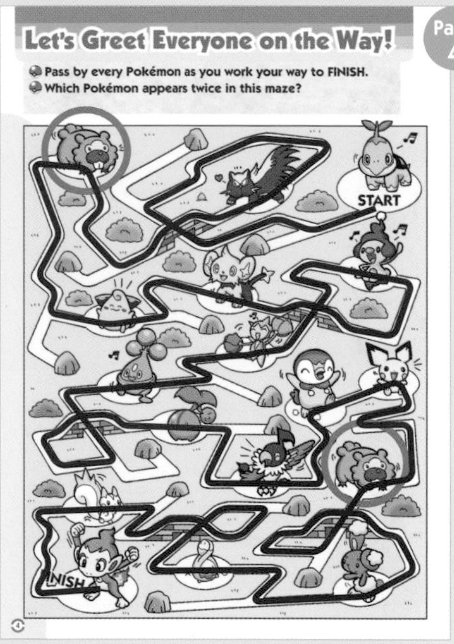

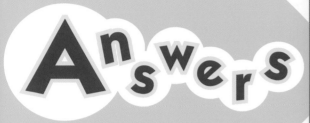

Let's Greet Everyone on the Way!
Page 4
Pass by every Pokémon as you work your way to FINISH.
Which Pokémon appears twice in this maze?
START

Bidoof appears twice in this maze.

Cross the Bridge and Finish!

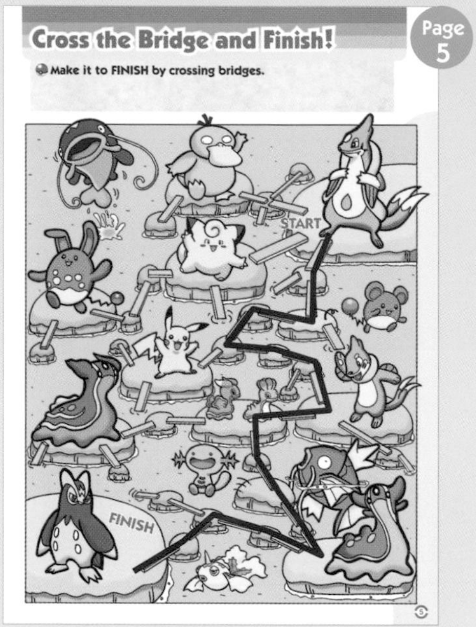

Cross the Bridge and Finish!
Page 5
Make it to FINISH by crossing bridges.
START
FINISH

Let's Climb the Rock Mountain!

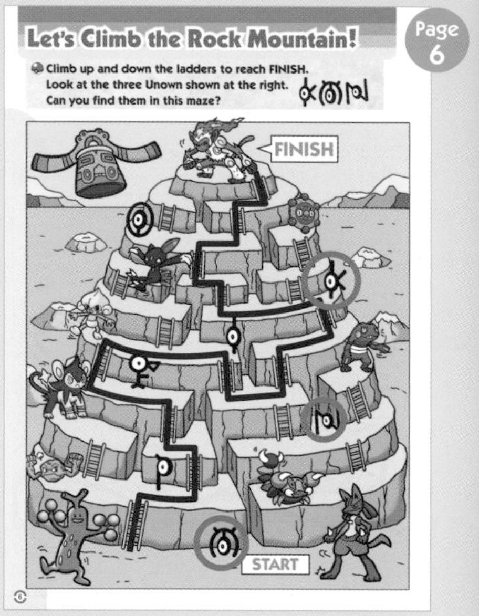

Let's Climb the Rock Mountain!
Page 6
Climb up and down the ladders to reach FINISH.
Look at the three Unown shown at the right.
Can you find them in this maze?
FINISH
START

The circled Unown are the ones you were looking for.

The Most Pokémon

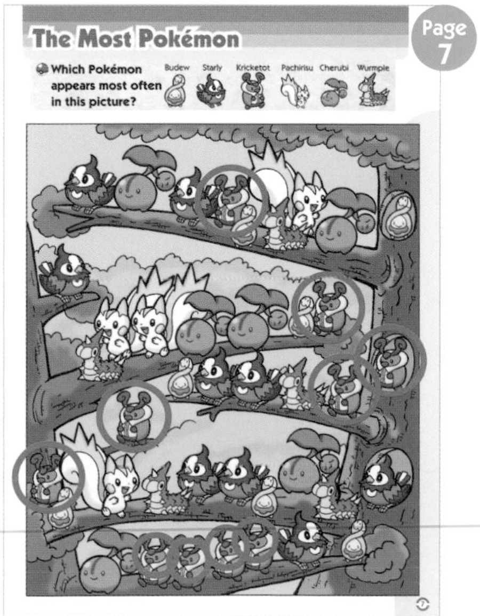

The Most Pokémon
Page 7
Which Pokémon appears most often in this picture?
Budew
Starly
Kricketot
Pachirisu
Cherubi
Wurmple

Kricketot appears more often than the others. There are ten Kricketot.

Let's Avoid Gible!

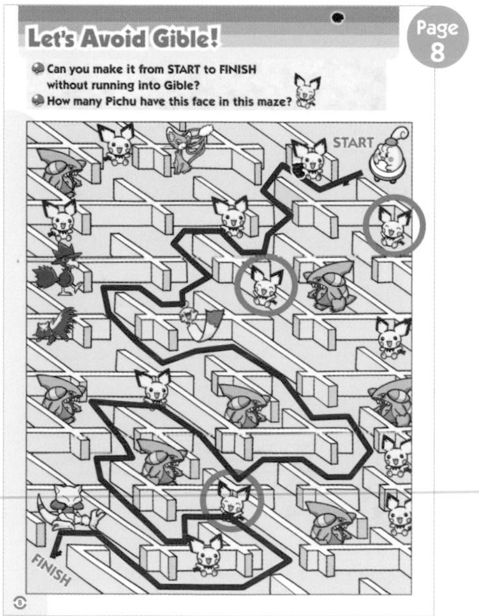

Let's Avoid Gible!
Page 8
Can you make it from START to FINISH without running into Gible?
How many Pichu have this face in this maze?
START
FINISH

There are three Pichu with smiley faces.

Let's Swim to Finish!

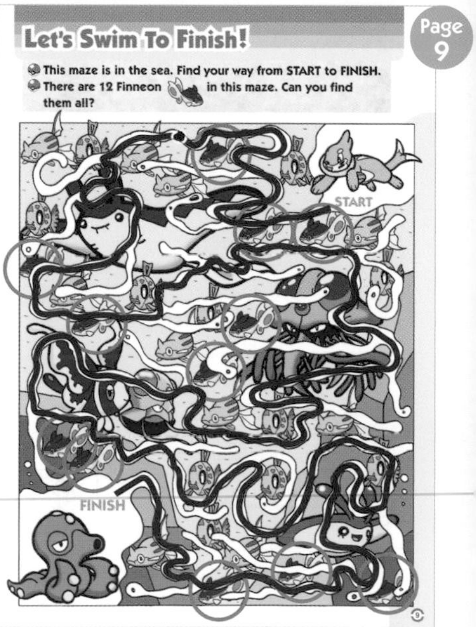

Let's Swim To Finish!
Page 9
This maze is in the sea. Find your way from START to FINISH.
There are 12 Finneon in this maze. Can you find them all?
START
FINISH

The Finneon are circled.

Find the Evolved Pokémon!

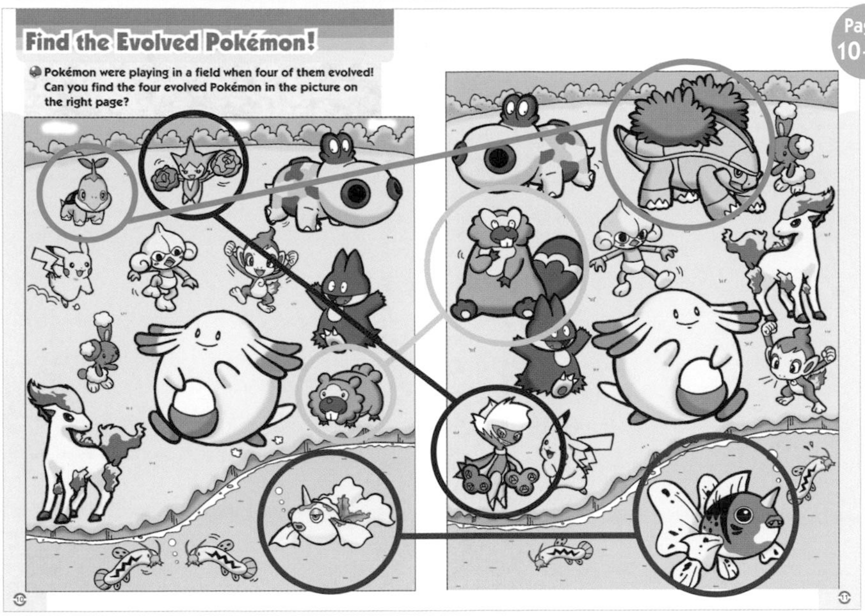

Find the Evolved Pokémon!
Pages 10–11
Pokémon were playing in a field when four of them evolved! Can you find the four evolved Pokémon in the picture on the right page?

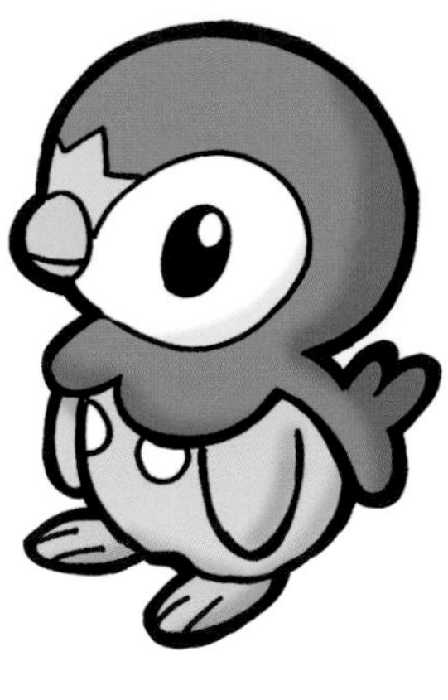

The following Pokémon evolved:

- Turtwig → Grotle
- Bidoof → Bibarel
- Roselia → Roserade
- Goldeen → Seaking

Cloud Maze

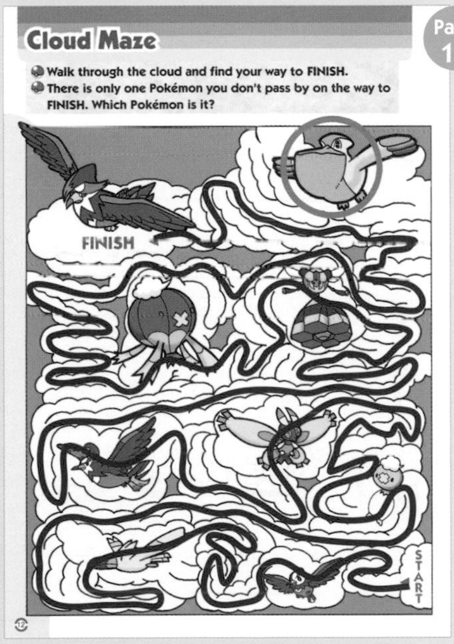

Cloud Maze
Page 12
Walk through the cloud and find your way to FINISH.
There is only one Pokémon you don't pass by on the way to FINISH. Which Pokémon is it?
FINISH
START

You don't pass by Pelipper.

Fun with Japanese!

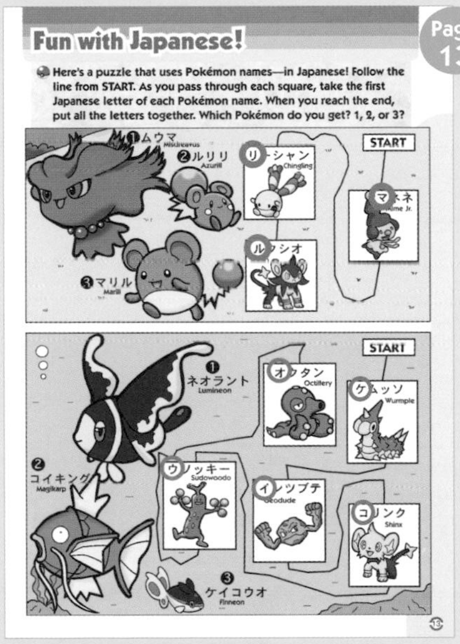

Fun with Japanese!
Page 13
Here's a puzzle that uses Pokémon names—in Japanese! Follow the line from START. As you pass through each square, take the first Japanese letter of each Pokémon name. When you reach the end, put all the letters together. Which Pokémon do you get? 1, 2, or 3?
START
START

Top: The answer is ❸, Marill.
Bottom: The answer is ❸, Finneon.

Let's Walk Around Budew!

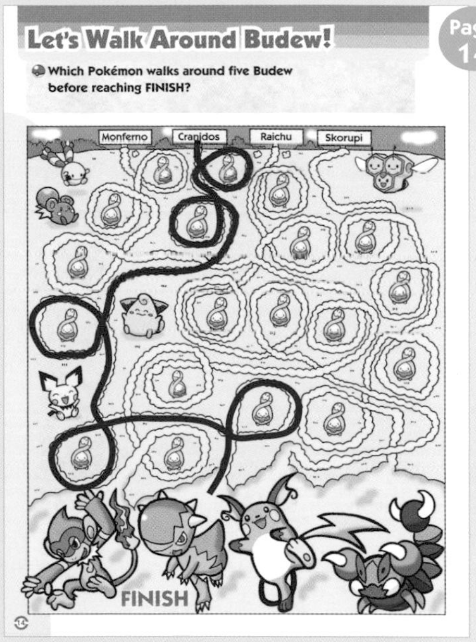

Let's Walk Around Budew!
Page 14
Which Pokémon walks around five Budew before reaching FINISH?
Monferno
Cranidos
Raichu
Skorupi
FINISH

Cranidos walked around five Budew.

Let's Play a Japanese Word Game!

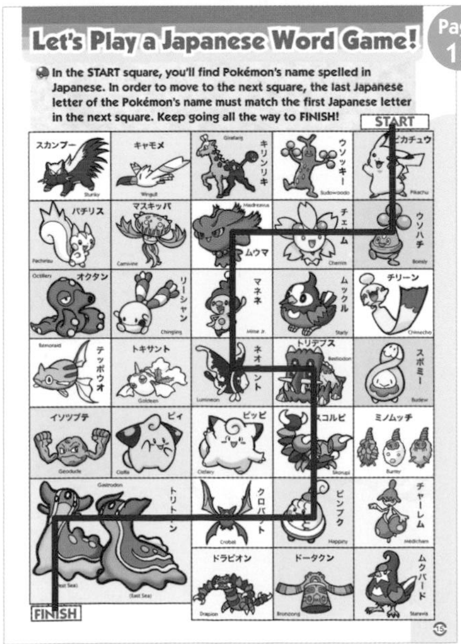

Let's Play a Japanese Word Game!
Page 15
In the START square, you'll find Pokémon's name spelled in Japanese. In order to move to the next square, the last Japanese letter of the Pokémon's name must match the first Japanese letter in the next square. Keep going all the way to FINISH!
START
FINISH

One Less or One More

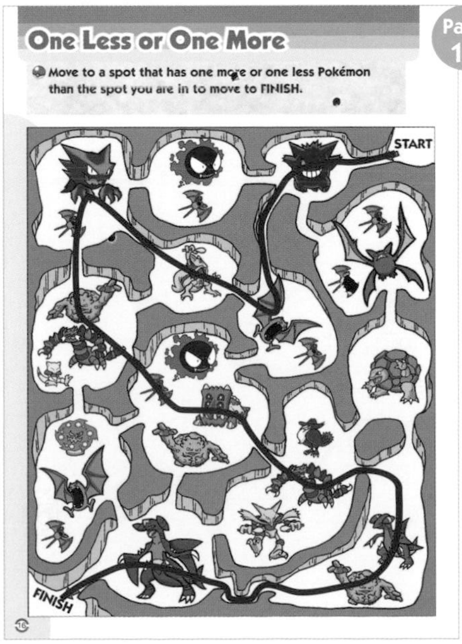

One Less or One More
Page 16
Move to a spot that has one more or one less Pokémon than the spot you are in to move to FINISH.
START
FINISH

Who Will Collect the Most Nuts?

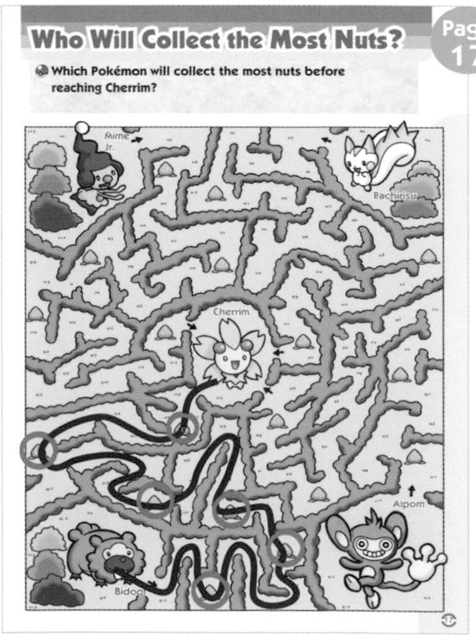

Who Will Collect the Most Nuts?
Page 17
Which Pokémon will collect the most nuts before reaching Cherrim?
Mime Jr.
Pachirisu
Cherrim
Aipom
Bidoof

Bidoof collected the most nuts.
He found six.

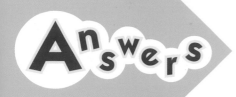

Answers

Pikachu's 100,000 Volts!

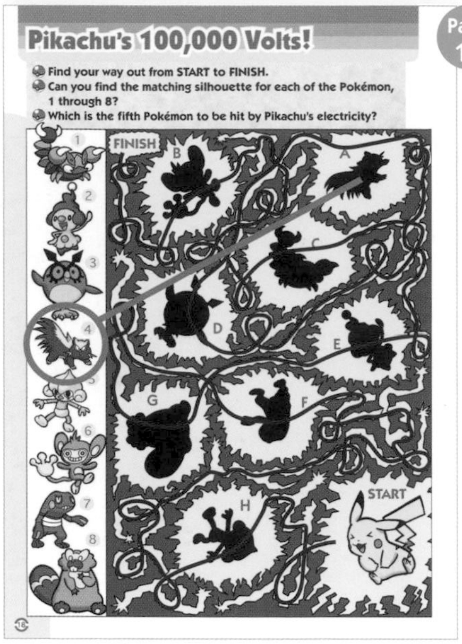

Pikachu's 100,000 Volts!
Page 18
Find your way out from START to FINISH.
Can you find the matching silhouette for each of the Pokémon, 1 through 8?
Which is the fifth Pokémon to be hit by Pikachu's electricity?
FINISH
START

A is ❹, Stunky
B is ❻, Aipom
C is ❶, Skorupi
D is ❸, Hoothoot
E is ❷, Mime Jr.
F is ❼, Croagunk
G is ❽, Bibarel
H is ❺, Meditite

Stunky is the fifth Pokémon to be hit by Pikachu's volts.

Let's Move In Order!

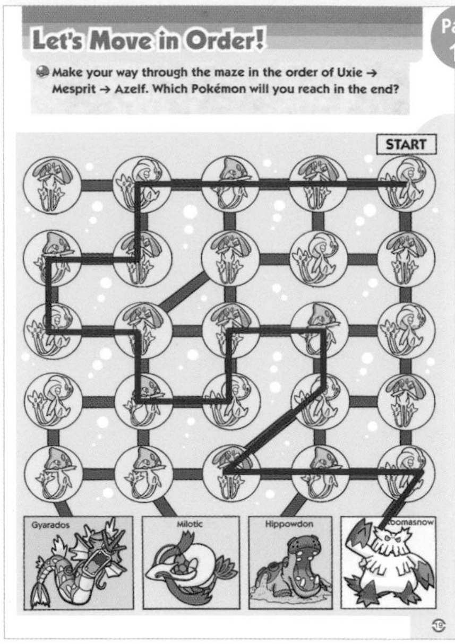

Let's Move in Order!
Page 19
Make your way through the maze in the order of Uxie → Mesprit → Azelf. Which Pokémon will you reach in the end?
START
Gyarados
Milotic
Hippowdon
Abomasnow

Who's Missing?

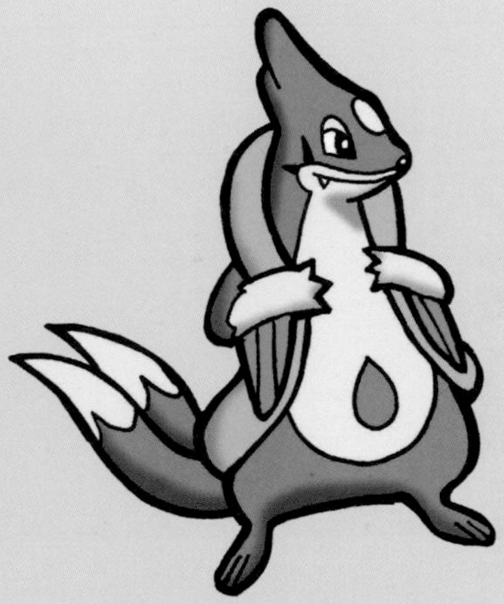

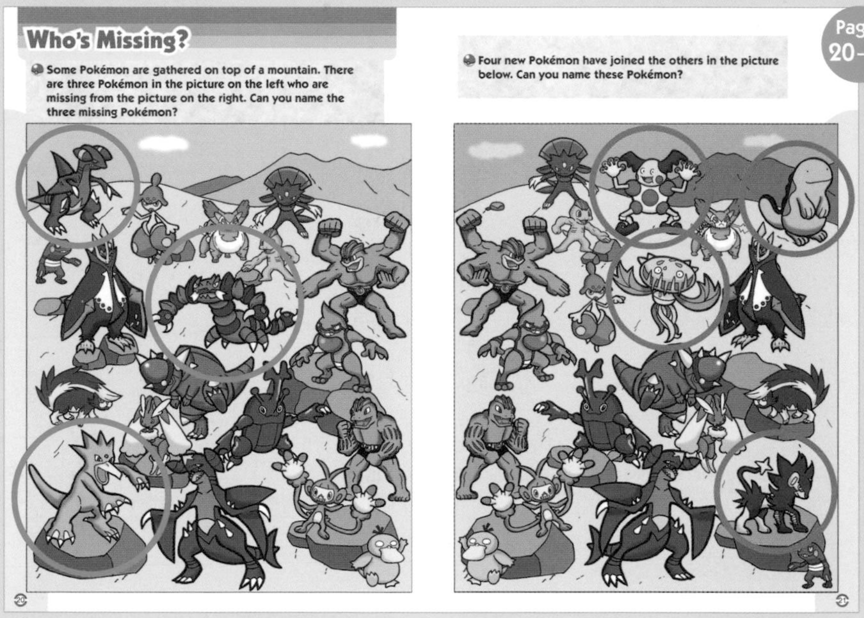

Who's Missing?
Pages 20–21
Some Pokémon are gathered on top of a mountain. There are three Pokémon in the picture on the left who are missing from the picture on the right. Can you name the three missing Pokémon?
Four new Pokémon have joined the others in the picture below. Can you name these Pokémon?

The three missing Pokémon are Gabite, Drapion and Golduck. They are in the blue circles.

The four Pokémon who came later are Quagsire, Mr. Mime, Carnivine and Luxray. They are in the orange circles.

Brick Maze

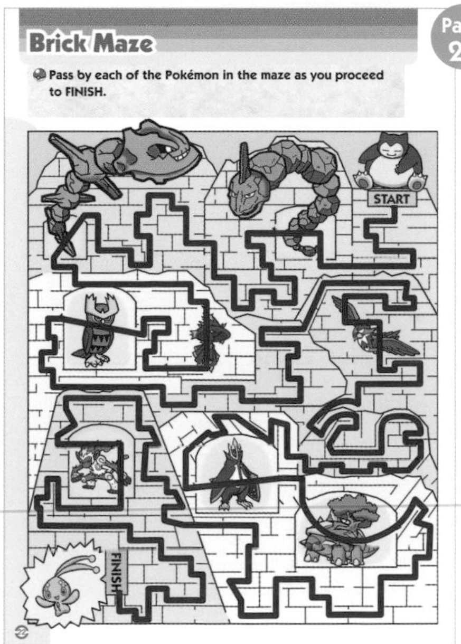

Brick Maze
Page 22
Pass by each of the Pokémon in the maze as you proceed to FINISH.
START
FINISH

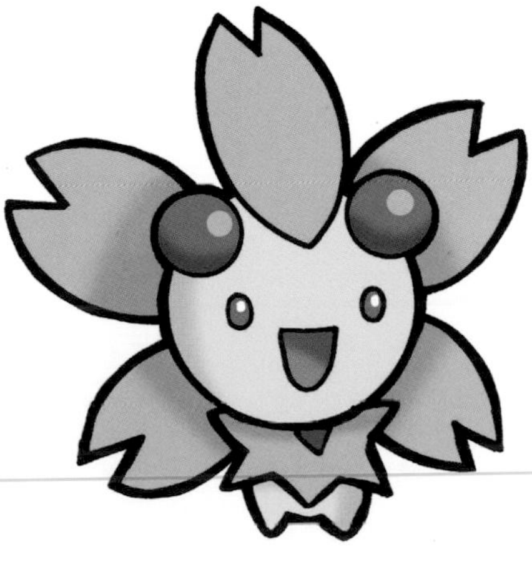

Who Will Meet the Most Pokémon?

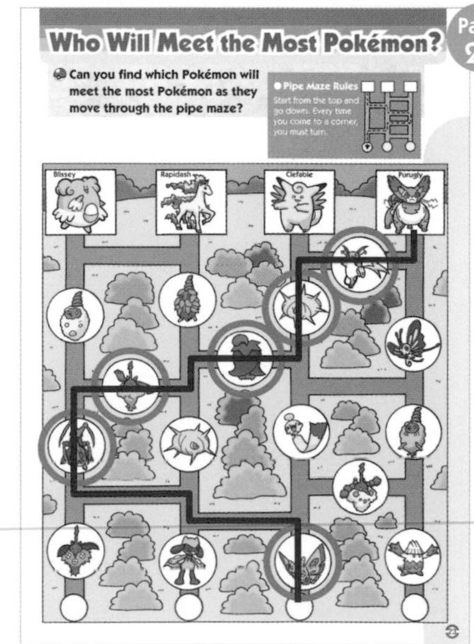

Who Will Meet the Most Pokémon?
Page 23
Can you find which Pokémon will meet the most Pokémon as they move through the pipe maze?
Pipe Maze Rules
Start from the top and go down. Every time you come to a corner, you must turn.
Blissey
Rapidash
Clefable
Purugly

Purugly met the most Pokémon on the way to FINISH. Purugly met six Pokémon.